"What's the highest tower?"
BeeGee asked

"It sounds like a riddle, but..." She hesitated when Dan's expression turned murderous.

"Who's the blabbermouth? The highest tower, huh?"

"Sorry I asked. I didn't mean to pry."

"Love is the highest tower." Dan bit off each word. "Let's go."

Without waiting, he was out of the restaurant and stalking to the truck. BeeGee hurried after him, totally bewildered at his reaction and slightly miffed. He was usually so cool, so controlled. Why love—or the mere mention of it—would bend him out of shape mystified her.

BeeGee turned to glare at Dan. "Never mind!"

"I do mind," he said in a more subdued voice. "It's kind of a private family joke. The highest tower is love and once you scale it, you can't get down. You can't even fall off if it's really love. You just stay there, at the very pinnacle.

Dear Reader,

Although our culture is always changing, the desire to love and be loved is a constant in every woman's heart. Silhouette Romances reflect that desire, sweeping you away with books that will make you laugh and cry, poignant stories that will move you time and time again.

This year we're featuring Romances with a playful twist. Remember those fun-loving heroines who always manage to get themselves into tricky predicaments? You'll enjoy reading about their escapades in Silhouette Romances by Brittany Young, Debbie Macomber, Annette Broadrick and Rita Rainville.

We're also publishing Romances by many of your all-time favorites such as Ginna Gray, Dixie Browning, Laurie Paige and Joan Hohl. Your overwhelming reaction to these authors has served as a touchstone for us, and we're pleased to bring you more books with Silhouette's distinctive medley of charm, wit and—above all—*romance*. I hope you enjoy this book, and the many stories to come.

Sincerely,

Rosalind Noonan
Senior Editor
SILHOUETTE BOOKS

ANN HURLEY
The Highest Tower

Silhouette Romance

Published by Silhouette Books New York

America's Publisher of Contemporary Romance

SILHOUETTE BOOKS
300 E. 42nd St., New York, N.Y. 10017

Copyright © 1986 by Ann Salerno

Distributed by Pocket Books

ISBN: 0-373-08408-0

First Silhouette Books printing January 1986

10 9 8 7 6 5 4 3 2 1

America's Publisher of Contemporary Romance

Printed in the U.S.A.

ANN HURLEY

sprang from a family chock-full of lawyers, teachers and scientists. After a long stint teaching literature and creative writing, Ann realized that she wanted to *write* most of all. Although she has traveled extensively, she chose to settle in Albuquerque, New Mexico, where she frequently walks across the mesa west of the city for a glimpse of the Sandias and the majestic Rio Grande.

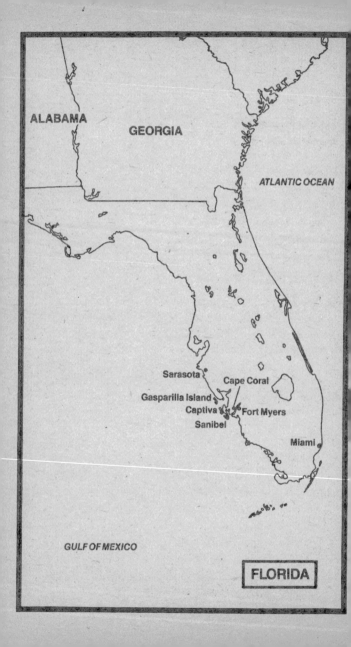

Chapter One

It was hot. Under the roof's overhang, it was even hotter. BeeGee Chambers was miserably aware of the itch and trickle of sweat every time she lifted her arm to stroke more white paint on the soffit and fascia. Half an hour, she figured as she peered down the final length of the Clifton house; no more than a hour, tops, and she'd be done.

The screen door opened with a shrill metallic protest from ancient hinges and a thin voice with its own quaver of age drifted upward.

"Please take a break now," urged Mrs. Clifton. "Lemonade or iced tea?"

BeeGee ducked her head out and canted back slightly from the aluminum ladder. There was a hint of ocean breeze, the best relief from Florida's sum-

mer heat and humidity. She grinned down at her customer, pulling off a paint-speckled scarf and stuffing
it into the back pocket of her faded jeans.

"I'm ready to jump off for anything cold right
about now. Thanks, Mrs. C. Whatever you have
handy is fine."

The air stirred again. BeeGee ran her fingers
through the dense mass of short, dark brown curls that
the bandanna had flattened. One sneakered toe felt for
the rung to make the descent but BeeGee stopped herself, staring across the tiny front yard and the street to
Art's gas station.

There wasn't much tourist trade in Fort Myers in
July and the town was small enough to pay attention
to out-of-season newcomers. A new blue Bronco
pulled in first, followed by two sleek silver trailers.
BeeGee saw the tall man get out of the Bronco and
wave the others behind the gas pumps toward the deserted rest area. From her vantage point, BeeGee
studied the group and discarded her first guess. Lots
of Gypsies—the real Romany Gypsies—used this route
following their annual trek along the coast to and from
their winter haven. Whoever these visitors were, they
weren't Gypsies.

The man had walked with an easy athletic stride
back to see Art and took off his baseball cap to rub his
sleeve across his brow. He was very blond. The sun,
flashing white-gold on his head, dazzled BeeGee for a
second. When Art gestured to the north, the man half
turned and BeeGee was reminded of a Viking movie
she'd suffered through. This stranger was as big and

handsome, tanned and light haired as the unbelievable, inarticulate hero of that epic.

Her thirst was greater than her curiosity. BeeGee
climbed down when Mrs. Clifton reappeared, setting
a tray on a round wrought-iron table. The elderly
woman held out a huge plastic tumbler beaded with
moisture and filled with ice.

"Here we are, dear. Just the breather you need."
Mrs. Clifton's gnarled forefinger pointed to the bright
red letters on BeeGee's white T-shirt. They pro-
claimed BeeGee Can Do It. "Not at breakneck speed
in July," amended the woman.

"Whenever and wherever there's work," said
BeeGee on a more grateful than boastful note.

Her customer nodded agreement and looked ap-
provingly at the glistening, still-wet evidence of a hard
day's work. More and more of the local residents were
beginning to trust the motto that decorated the side of
BeeGee's twelve-year-old pickup truck, as well as a
wardrobe of T-shirts. After two years of struggle to get
a home-repair business going, BeeGee believed more
than ever that she could do it.

There was another scrape-and-paint job scheduled
after the Cliftons and a minor roofing problem and a
sidewalk patch with a possibility of a patio order. It
wouldn't bring in the riches of Peru—sometimes her
schedule moved in fits and starts, just like the bat-
tered Ford—but it was hers. The odd notion of a re-
liable Handy Andy being a five-foot-one woman had
finally ceased to be so odd. The same people who had
predicted disaster when she'd left a good accounting

job now called her to mend their picket fences or put up a new television antenna.

"Now, BeeGee, about the money..." Mrs. Clifton cleared her throat and tried to sound firm. "I know what you said before but if it works any hardship on you to wait so long..."

BeeGee swallowed the last gulp of tea hastily, anxious to interrupt before Mrs. Clifton embarrassed either of them. There was no hardship of BeeGee's comparable to living on a very small fixed income. She insisted there was no rush for immediate payment and scurried back up the ladder to force an end to the discussion.

She went to work with only an occasional glance over at the gas station. There were others milling around now. The tall blonde was on the pay phone and another man was chatting with the station's owner while a small towheaded child tugged at him.

"Hey, there! BeeGee?"

When she turned slightly toward the unfamiliar male voice, BeeGee saw only his grin at first. It was a very wide and toothy smile, the open look of someone sure that his greeting would be returned. Yet it was the stranger—the very same man she had been peeping at from her perch.

BeeGee nodded and smiled back. Confronted with such a confident, expectant expression, it was next to impossible not to smile. "That's me. Ruth Chambers, actually, but BeeGee will do."

"*Can* do, according to your own advertising," he pointed out. He was inside the low picket fence,

reaching up to shake her hand before the final sylla-
ble floated away in the hot air. "I'm Dan. Dan
Greening. The man over at the filling station suggested I stroll over and see you. We seem to have hit a
snag..."

She stretched to take the big, well-shaped hand he
offered. "And I fix snags," BeeGee finished for him.
"Well, I claim to fix everything, even things I'm not
sure of."

He laughed, and it was a contagious sound, as warm
as the flesh she kept gripping in a peculiar, awkward
hold. Up close, Dan Greening was even more impressive.

"That's exactly what's needed." He glanced at her
fingers still laced in his, slowly retrieved his hand and
hooked his thumb in a belt loop. Eyes as blue as a
shallow lagoon narrowed slightly in his strong, tanned
face. "You see, my brother and his family and I were
headed for Tallahassee but it looks as if we might have
to stop here for a few days."

"I don't fix trailers," BeeGee put in, puzzled. "If
Art can't work on the problem, there's a fellow in Fort
Myers Beach who might."

"Oh, no," Dan said with a quick shake of his head.
"We need a doctor, not a mechanic. Actually, it's
Judy, my sister-in-law. When we were in Miami she
found out she was pregnant, but she's feeling weird.
We need someone to check her out."

BeeGee shifted her weight from side to side and
found it easier to understand him if she paid strict attention to his words, not his bright eyes. Suddenly the

confusion resolved itself. "Oh, I can guide you to the clinic. It's off the beaten path, I know."

She wondered how much Art had said about her, besides the fact that Doc Alden was her father. It was a silly thought. What did it matter? This man was only passing through, not sticking around.

"Great, thanks. Let me go tell Alex and Judy and see how they want to handle this. Someone's got to watch Kip and make arrangements for a place to set up the trailers."

It was ridiculous for her to keep staring at him, dying to ask if he had ever been in a Grade Z movie with a battle-ax and horned helmet. BeeGee swiped at the remaining boards and a sizable blob of white paint flew off the bristles and landed on her chin.

"No rush," Dan cautioned with another nice laugh. "This isn't a dire emergency. I can wait until you finish decorating the house."

"And myself," BeeGee added ruefully, smearing the paint away and depositing it on the worn, streaked leg of her jeans.

She was aware to the second of how long Dan Greening stood there, smiling. When he let himself out of the Cliftons' yard and headed back across the street, she made a concerted effort to keep her brown eyes on the job at hand. It sure didn't take much, she decided, to stir up excitement in Fort Myers in the summer. A block party, a supermarket opening or a new face were big doings.

If these wayfarers were from Miami and spent any time here, they'd laugh themselves silly or die of boredom. Once the annual flock of tourists—the snowbirds—left, this town slowed its heartbeat down to a low murmur and fell asleep. It was a Rip Van Winkle place.

She stowed the paint and ladder in her truck and let Mrs. Clifton know she was done. The woman's thanks followed her even after the screen door rattled closed.

"See you soon," BeeGee called back over her shoulder. She nearly ended up in Mrs. Clifton's old tire planter among the marigolds and amarantha when she collided with a very solid, warm wall. It was Dan Greening's chest. His quick reflexes managed to keep her upright. Her own klutziness flustered her. His dazzling display of white teeth was totally unnerving.

"I usually look where I'm going," she said lamely. "I was just coming over to get you."

"Well, I like to meet people halfway," he teased. "I don't usually expect to sweep them off their feet."

You have the potential for it, BeeGee almost said. Dan would be better than a broom if she counted only good looks, a friendly smile and a strong steady grip for a whole lot.

"Falling off high ladders...or for strange men...isn't one of my problems." She smiled to take any sting out of her words and pushed back an errant damp curl with her paint-speckled hand.

This time around he was the one holding on, reluctant to take his hand off her upper arm. Maybe he thought she was always this clumsy. He gave BeeGee a sweeping glance that was too quick to be offensive and let go of her abruptly. It didn't take long to survey her, she knew. "Big as a minute, light as a feather," Doc Alden always said.

"You don't look like a lady with too many problems," Dan remarked as they headed out the gate. "Agile, accomplished and pretty, right?"

He was making fun of her. She was sure of it. Even in clean clothes, BeeGee thought of herself as only passably attractive in a healthy, Brownie Scout way. In grubbies, punctuated with a pint of white paint and a dirty face, she guessed she looked like a short, silly troll.

"This is our local angel, Alex," Dan said, introducing her to his older brother. "Her dad runs the clinic. Is Judy ready to go?"

The family resemblance was striking. Alex was only slightly shorter, slightly burlier than Dan. The little boy, scooting in and out and around the two men's legs, could have belonged to either of them; he was a very wriggly miniature with white-blond hair.

"She's lying down inside. Let's go see," said Alex, grabbing his son before he darted off. "I think I'll take Kip for a new pair of sneakers at that department store we passed on the way into town. He needs to run off some of this energy."

"Markham's," supplied BeeGee. "I used to work there." She tickled the five-year-old's ribs and whispered conspiratorially to him to be sure to ask for a comic book and a free pair of extra shoelaces. "Make sure you get all the freebies, just like a native."

She stood inside the trailer's door while Alex conferred quietly with his wife. Judy was stretched out on the couch. For Gypsies, BeeGee mused, they traveled in fine style. The interior was spacious and beautifully decorated. A quick, unobtrusive peek around revealed a modern kitchen and all the comforts of any nice home.

"I'm sorry to put everyone to so much trouble," apologized Judy as she levered herself off the couch and came over. She, too, towered over BeeGee and her handshake revealed calluses and strength. "I'm not exactly a delicate flower like you," she added with a likable grin.

"Don't let appearances fool you," said BeeGee. "And it's no trouble. I'm finished for the day."

Judy had a round, open face and an open manner to match. During the short ride she did most of the talking while BeeGee was required only to direct Dan down the palm-lined boulevard and point at which bridge to take.

"Oh, I'm a nervous wreck," wailed Judy as they made the final turn to the clinic. She clung to BeeGee as if they were sisters. "I want everything to be all right. I want this baby. I want..."

Dan patted his sister-in-law's arm awkwardly. "You're fine. You're the woman of steel, Judy. Hang in there!"

The Alden Clinic looked like a cozy old home identical to its neighbors, which was exactly what it was. Doc Alden had practiced in the community since his graduation from medical school nearly forty years earlier. There had been no need—or money—to build a more impressive structure then; the mere presence of a doctor sufficed.

BeeGee led the way up the flower-lined walk, moving a tricycle out of the way. Doc was of the school, she explained, that treated everybody, specialized in nothing and would even stitch a dog's torn ear if the vet in town was swamped. He wasn't fancy, just good.

"It's nothing," Judy kept saying, as if willing her own diagnosis.

Doc was too busy to stop and chat, even briefly, this afternoon. He kissed BeeGee and took Judy back with him to one of the recently remodeled examining rooms. There was little to do but wait.

"Did you have a hand in this?" asked Dan after listening for a while to BeeGee's banter. "You do carpentry and painting and what all?"

"Mostly what all," she admitted. "I was a souvenir salesperson, a bookkeeper, a waitress after high school. I didn't love any of those jobs, and once I started classes at our community college I wanted desperately to do something to counteract the sitting-there-studying fidgets."

"Jill-of-all-trades? Does it keep you busy enough?"

Dan didn't seem surprised or amused at all. He was really interested, leaning toward her so he didn't miss a word above the squalls of an infant. His questions came fast and were very specific, much more than idle curiosity. After he insisted on knowing all the services she offered and what she charged, BeeGee wondered if he was going to offer her a job.

There was muffled laughter and Judy emerged, smiling and with a touch of color back in her face. Doc Alden gave her a wink and waved her off as another patient came in.

"It's nothing, I know," BeeGee blurted out as they left.

"It's a dinner invitation," Judy replied, somewhat dazed. "I never met a doctor like your father before...."

"Adoptive father," corrected BeeGee. "But, yes, Doc's quite a character."

On the way back to Art's, Judy filled them in, knowing she would have to recite the whole story again for Alex and Kip. The diagnosis was fatigue, the prescription was to take it easy for a while and the prognosis was a new Greening in six months. Nothing dire, Judy had been assured, but she couldn't keep up with her work for the next few months.

"And what is your work?" inquired BeeGee. It suddenly occurred to her that she has been answering all the questions, not asking any.

"Why, we..." started Judy, but Dan cut her off, wanting to know about the dinner she mentioned. "Oh, yes, Doc Alden wanted all of us to show up at his house tonight. I thought maybe he was worried that we were down-and-out but he gave me a real argument and a hard sell."

BeeGee laughed at Judy's bewilderment. "That's him. We've had circus performers, tourists, rangers from the wildlife haven and half the immediate world drop in for dinner. Doc is kind of a people collector.

He meets someone who interests him and he has to find out about him."

"That's a nice hobby," commented Dan. "We do much the same thing except we go out and find interesting people…like you, like Doc." It was his turn to laugh and Judy joined in. "One of the benefits of not being tied down is not running out of new faces."

"That's your work?" BeeGee was incredulous. "Are you a casting company on wheels?"

She never got a reply. They were back to the starting point and Kip was leaping up and down at the sight of the Bronco. Well, it could wait for dinner, she assumed. From the sound of the plans Alex and Dan were busy hatching, it didn't sound as if this caravan would be pulling out immediately.

Whoever and whatever these people were, they were a happy family. There weren't any grunts and groans over the unexpected changes and no complaints. There was instant bustle and efficiency as they prepared to find hookups for the trailers.

"I'd better get going. I'll see you later." BeeGee was aware of her own inexplicable reluctance to leave. She'd done what she was supposed to, and now she was hanging around.

"Thanks for everything," Judy said, and came over to plant an unexpected kiss on BeeGee's cheek. Alex echoed the sentiment and the little boy threw his arms around one of BeeGee's legs and squeezed her.

Their effusive gratitude was embarrassing. She hadn't done anything noteworthy, in her estimation, but the feeling got worse when Dan walked her to her own pickup.

He kept his hand on the truck as he ducked his head slightly so they were face-to-face when BeeGee was settled in the driver's seat. His eyes held hers for a long minute and he appeared to mull over a thought before he spoke.

"Thanks, angel," he said finally. "I've got an idea I really want to talk to you about. It just occurred to me after seeing the clinic that Judy...well, let it jell and I'll proposition you after dinner."

Her face reflected her shock. A twinkle crept into his blue eyes and Dan reached in, tugging a single dark curl to chide her.

"Shame on you for that thought," he scolded. "I don't give warnings for dishonorable intentions, you better believe."

"No, men usually don't." She switched the ignition on and gunned the engine to cover the less than steady sound of her voice and her confusion. "By, Dan."

One second, BeeGee had been drinking in the sight of him, loath to leave. The next, she couldn't wait to escape his knowing expression and casual teasing. The choice of pet name he'd called her should have tipped her off, she reflected as the truck labored onto the causeway. It was the soft sound of it, the shape of "angel" on his wide, sensuous mouth that made her remember caution and common sense.

She was not an angel. She was not even reasonably intelligent if she let herself go all silly because a handsome man smiled at her. There was, most likely, a trail of goggle-eyed, bubble-headed women with broken hearts in the wake of Mr. Dan Greening. Tonight, she'd ask the questions and figure out if he—or any idea he had—was worth another minute of her time.

Chapter Two

Not a minute too soon," Emma Alden's cheerful voice rang from the front of the house. "The food's ready, so we can avoid standing around making polite chat. Now, this little fellow is Kip, right?"

BeeGee set down the final place setting with a thump and shook her head in amazement. Her adoptive mother should host diplomatic parties in Washington, she thought. Emma had a talent for assembling dinners for any number on a moment's notice, making odd assemblages of people feel friendly and full and doing it as if it required no effort.

"Hi, again," said Judy as the Greenings were herded into the dining room. "Point me toward the kitchen. Kip is going to show me how he washes his hands...with soap this time."

Mrs. Alden took care of seating arrangements in short order. She shooed Dan down the table to sit next to Doc and across from BeeGee and claimed a grandmother's right to put the youngest dinner guest next to herself.

"We won't play 'What's My Line,' Em, because you'd never guess these nice folks' occupation," Doc announced. "I don't believe I've met steeplejacks before. A rare, almost extinct profession—like horseshoeing."

"Oh, my!" Mrs. Alden was suitably impressed. "You all climb up and repair chimneys and steeples and such? What dangerous work!"

There was instant denial by the three Greening adults. Their work was exciting, even fun. They used old-fashioned rigging, ropes and pulleys, not scaffolds, but they felt completely safe, no matter how far off the ground they were. The need for steeplejacks, like blacksmiths, would always exist to some extent.

"If you can climb a tree, you can climb a tower," said Alex, helping himself to more pot roast. "We've been doing this for four years now and covered ten...no, eleven states. Not one serious accident. And we've painted and repaired an awful lot of high trestle bridges, factory chimneys, water towers and churches."

Dan added a personal boast. "Anything man builds, I can climb."

BeeGee was quiet, taking in every word and sorting out all this new information. She caught Dan's amusement at her wide-eyed interest and thought about their meeting that afternoon.

"No wonder I got the fish eye from you earlier," she said. "Here you were, an expert on heights, watching my not so fancy footwork on a ladder at the Cliftons and criticizing my form."

"Not at all," denied Dan, and Alex snorted.

"My brother never criticizes a lady's form. He tends to enjoy it, regardless of size and shape."

BeeGee digested that kernel easily. It followed that an unmarried man, constantly on the move, would have a love-'em-and-leave-'em policy. Dan didn't bother to argue, saying that variety was the spice of all their lives.

Judy seconded his motion. "I always wanted to travel," she explained. "I used to dream about cities with sunny climates during subzero winter in Detroit. We're all from Michigan originally."

"I don't care where we are or how many pretty girls are there," Alex chimed in, with a wink across the table at his wife. "For me, it's food. Eating oysters in New Orleans, Cuban food in Miami...and another piece of your key lime pie, Mrs. Alden, if you don't mind."

Before Alex could wax too eloquent on the subject, Judy suggested she might not be the only one who should watch her weight for a while. The rest of dinner was taken up with good-natured teasing and the easy-flowing conversation of a Sunday family gathering. Emma Alden lamented how rarely she got to spoil her own three grandchildren and managed to slip

Kip an extra dessert on the strength of her deprivation.

"Well, I know how Judy is supposed to spend the next week," sighed Doc, patting his paunch contentedly. "What are the rest of you planning? You can sun, swim or sit around and let your arteries harden like some of my patients."

Dan and Alex exchanged a quick glance. Thanking Mrs. Alden profusely, Dan excused himself, promising he'd be back after he ran one more errand. He leveled his startling blue eyes at BeeGee and asked her if she was in the mood for a short ride.

"You wouldn't want me to take a wrong turn and end up driving off one of those tricky bridges into the ocean or a swamp. Besides, there's that matter of a certain prop—" He caught himself and grinned. "Proposal, that is."

"You always were a fast worker," muttered Alex, and got a surprisingly dirty look from his younger brother.

"Oh, no," BeeGee said with unnecessary vehemence. She stood up and started clearing the table, despite Emma's quizzical stare and assurance that the dishes weren't going anyplace. She tugged down the cuffs of her yellow cotton shorts and dropped her voice slightly to take some of the sting out of her words. The last thing she was interested in was a fast worker who knew he was irresistible to women.

"I'm sure Dan won't get lost. Getting around sounds like one of his strong suits. You can take a piece of bread and leave a trail of crumbs to follow, if you're planning to return. I'll be right here.''

"Ruth's a regular little homebody," Doc Alden complained, without directing his comment to anyone in particular. "She'll hang around and fix the television before she'll go out on a date."

BeeGee groaned and swept out of the dining room clutching a stack of plates before Emma could join in or urge her to go. She waited until she heard the front door slam and felt fairly sure that she had seen the last of Dan Greening for the evening. He'd probably find one of the two local hangouts and what passed for fast living in Fort Myers.

Even if she dated frequently, BeeGee would have thought twice about getting too friendly with Dan Greening. Twice? More than that, she mused with a sigh of relief and regret. Too good-looking, too sure of himself, too...everything.

"Nice people," Emma said as BeeGee brought the last stack of dishes into the kitchen.

"Nice," she echoed.

"Good-looking family." Mrs. Alden smiled expectantly. "That Dan doesn't find you too hard on the eyes, either."

"Give it up," warned BeeGee. This conversational direction wasn't going to lead anywhere. She and Emma had had similar guarded encounters before on the very same subject: BeeGee and men, BeeGee and the lack of men in Fort Myers, BeeGee and her apparent disinterest in men. "Here today and gone tomorrow."

Emma gave a sniff of disapproval and looked down
her nose at BeeGee. The only effect it had was to send
her glasses sliding down to the tip of her nose, and
BeeGee had to push them back up in place. "It didn't
sound to me as though they were rushing off. Doc said
a week at least and maybe more. A week is seven
days...and nights. Plenty of time to find out if you
like someone, I'd think."

"Plenty of time to create heaven and earth, and that
was a one-shot deal, too." BeeGee started for the
quickest escape route, swiping a few carrot sticks on
her way out. "I already know I like him but that's as
far as it goes."

"What ever happened to the notion of romance?
Marriage? Love?" Emma moaned loudly, more to
herself than for BeeGee's benefit. Her only answer was
the loud snap and crunch of carrot before the café
doors swung closed.

Everyone but Dan was in the living room. Doc was
teaching Kip checkers while Judy and Alex were having coffee, quietly chatting about their changed plans.
It was a nice, quiet family scene and one BeeGee
wanted no part of. She didn't need to know more
about these people when everything they said or did
seemed to involve her more and more. She didn't even
want to like them as much as she already did.

The front porch was dark and cool. BeeGee settled
herself into her favorite wicker rocker and contemplated the evening sky through the surrounding
screens. There were still a few minutes left before the
sunset, still the patches of flamingo-pink and orange

shading into darkness. She'd watched it a thousand times from this exact spot and would, she hoped, see it many thousands more—just the same and always a little different.

The outlined palm-tree fronds turned to purple lace, then to black filigree. The flow of light from inside the house spilled out and drew the moths to the screening. They dipped and hovered, begging admittance, brushing powdery silken wings on the wire mesh.

"Mind if I join you?" Dan said from somewhere out in the darkness. "Everything's set with the trailers. It looks as though we even have a job lined up in some place called Cape Coral."

When BeeGee didn't reply, he took it as an invitation to come up on the porch and sprawl comfortably in the hanging glider. She could hear the hum of voices inside, the occasional laughter and word, but it was quiet out here and strangely tense inside her. Only the creak of the glider was a reminder for a few minutes that she wasn't alone.

Dan cleared his throat. "I got the feeling at dinner that you don't think much of our work. Funny, too, since we seem to be second cousins when it comes to business. Not many women do what you do."

BeeGee shrugged and realized he couldn't see the gesture. "The jobs sound fascinating. I can't cotton to the idea of always being on the road without a real home."

"We've got homes," he protested softly. "Pegasus and the Eagle, our trailers, and they beat the hell out of tract houses in Detroit."

Without prompting, Dan started on a brief history of the Greenings and how they got started as steeple-jacking Gypsies. He interested BeeGee, despite her resolution not to get drawn in. She tried to imagine him as a real-estate investor, complete with striped tie and three-piece suit, and failed. Alex had been the foreman for a construction firm when he met Judy.

"And what was she doing?" It was impossible not to warm up and relax with him. He had a way of talking as if they were old friends catching each other up on the news since they were last together. "No, let me guess. A bored legal secretary?"

"A tired third-grade teacher," said Dan with a laugh. "Another vaguely discontented soul looking for something better."

Something better? They'd all had good, steady and well-paying jobs, BeeGee thought. They'd had friends and relatives around them and a place to go every night. What could there be to leave? She didn't say it but Dan appeared to read her mind.

"You told me you didn't like selling souvenirs or keeping books for Markham's. Well, the pay was great but the rewards weren't there. We like the new places and faces, the way every job is different...."

"Like a sunset," added BeeGee. "The same event with different colors, sometimes spectacular and sometimes just pleasant but always good."

"Exactly." He nodded, and by now her eyes could discern his shape in the dimness. "A touch of adventure and a taste of danger only made it better, as far as we were concerned. We did a few trial runs around

Michigan and painted water towers, repaired chimneys. It was great!"

"And here you are," finished BeeGee, "with a tower in Cape Coral you didn't expect to paint and things down the road waiting. Always one more river to cross."

He caught the note of disapproval in her tone and remarked on it. She didn't feel like going to the trouble of explaining where it came from and switched Dan over to a safer topic. As long as the Greenings were stuck in Fort Myers, she suggested they might want to know what was around to see and do. Even as she was extolling the beauties of the west Florida coast, the islands to visit and the Thomas Edison home, her mind was turning over and over, racing through Dan's background.

Maybe he expected—or wanted—a sharing of confidences, an explanation of who and what Ruth Chambers was. She wasn't going to do that. She couldn't. If he thought she was a born-and-bred small-town girl with a provincial outlook, so be it! If she sounded like someone who had never ventured farther than a rooftop in her hometown, she wasn't prepared to set him straight. It had always been a disaster before when she unbent too far and was totally honest.

Dan's voice cut through the gloom and into her consciousness. He was chanting nonsense. "Billy Goat... Big Gremlin... Bubble Gum. I give up. What is it?"

"I give up, too. I have no idea what you're... Oh, my nickname!" BeeGee's chin rose as if he had challenged her, and her soft mouth assumed a pinched look. "Baby Girl. BeeGee stands for Baby Girl Chambers, the only name on my birth certificate."

Most people took the hint when they heard the cold front creep into her normally sunny voice. "What about Ruth?" prodded Dan when she fell silent. "When you were adopted, did the Aldens name you?"

She got up, flicked on the amber porch light and sat back down in her chair.

"Boy, you sure ask a lot of questions," she snapped, hoping to make this inquiry very short. "Yes, they did. Four years ago, when I was seventeen, but a new name doesn't stick as well as the old tried and true. You know my age and I'm five foot two and I have all my own teeth. Anything else?"

He made the glider squeak so shrilly she knew she would remember to oil it in the morning. She waited, expecting him to get up and hotfoot it off the porch after her little show of nastiness. Instead of being put off or warned, he found it amusing and chuckled to himself.

"I'd bet you a dollar that you aren't over five one and those teeth are awfully sharp. I may have a deal you can sink them into, BeeGee."

"Proposition time," she said evenly. "I didn't forget. And I've lost fifty cents if you have a tape measure handy."

When they laughed together, the sound was very pleasant. It filled the whole space and gradually drifted away on the evening wind but there was a certain warmth left behind.

"It looks as if we can help each other," Dan began. "The water-tower job is a few days' work. Without Judy, we're shorthanded and I was thinking you might want to give steeplejacking a shot. The pay is good."

He mentioned the figure he and Alex charged for their service and BeeGee held her breath. They made more for a few days than she grossed in a very full week. She gnawed on her bottom lip and wondered what it would feel like to be able to pay all her bills on time this month.

"I have some commitments," she said, "and some possibles. My regular customers come first."

"Of course they do. We can work out a schedule that's fair for all of us."

So much agreement in so soothing a tone made her suspicious. "Wait a minute. If this is such a breeze, why do you need me? You and Alex could do it together and fatten your share. It might take an extra day, sure..."

"We don't know how long we're here for. The quicker we do it, the better." Dan's voice changed to a slower, insinuating drawl. "Maybe I was wrong. Maybe you aren't feisty enough for high work. Yeah, you can hold a brush or roller and stand on a ladder but there are a lot of painters who are afraid of heights. Real height."

She knew exactly what he was doing. The I-dare-you ploy wasn't even thinly disguised. Hanging off a water tower was hardly a game, and if not many painters did it, there were plenty of good reasons for her not to do it.

"Fixing is my specialty," she said. "Not falling, not flying. The money would come in handy but—"

"You're right," interrupted Dan. He got up and stood at the screen, his back to her. The golden glow made him look like a bronze statue, larger than life. The muscles in his forearms were sharply delineated, the broadness of his shoulders accentuated by the dim light. "It's not for everyone. Women in particular. At the risk of sounding sexist, I take back the offer. Judy is one in a million, most likely. It's hard, dirty and dangerous work...."

"Hey, I could do it." said BeeGee rather tartly. "And you are sexist, buddy. 'If man built it, I can climb it' is pure macho stuff and you know it."

He glanced back over his shoulder at her. "Really? And what about your advertising slogan? BeeGee Can Do It. Feminist talk, no action. You can put hinges on a gate or nail up a mailbox."

When he was daring her, she knew it and resisted. When he made the job sound so easy, she was on guard. Now Dan was being perfectly reasonable and BeeGee was furious.

"I'll do it," she said, "just to show you I can. At the price you mentioned, of course."

He turned to her, folded his arms across his chest and leaned back. "I took back my offer. You're right again. Alex and I will do it without any extra help."

How could someone keep telling her she was right and still make her crazy? BeeGee changed tactics. She smiled sweetly, relaxed by sheer force of will and hoped she appeared very small and feminine.

"I'm sure you could do it alone—if you had to, Dan. Being a woman alone in business is very difficult. So-o-o difficult at times." She tipped her head to one side, trying to look like a sparrow, not a vulture. "I can hardly find the time to learn new skills, advertise my business and do all the work. It would be a big help to partner with you and Alex. I might be able to get the local paper to give you—"

He laughed. He laughed so hard BeeGee thought the Aldens and the other Greenings would race out to see if the Marx Brothers had dropped by for a visit. "You're better at being feisty than phony," he managed to gasp out. "That was the worst 'poor little me' act I ever saw."

"Well, everything I said was true," BeeGee said sheepishly. "It was the way I said it...."

She didn't mind that he enjoyed her act and she didn't mind getting caught, she discovered. She giggled, too, because she was fairly sure he was laughing at her inept performance of feminine wiles, not her. And he was going to agree.

"All right, all right." Dan nodded. "You can prove whatever you want to everybody else and yourself. We can see how it goes the first day. Deal?"

She beamed at him. "Deal!"

Dan took a step toward her and covered almost the whole porch in that one easy stride. "Is your word your bond or do we seal this with a kiss?'' he asked in a very light way.

He was joking. She knew he was joking but the knowledge didn't stop her smile from freezing on her face. Looming over her, Dan was not easy to ignore. Even more distressing than his banter was the flicker of a feeling in her. She could put him in his place, she was sure. But she felt a brief twinge of regret that it was only a joke. BeeGee doused the little firefly light without hesitation.

"This is business. Strictly business," she reminded him. "Unless you make it a practice to kiss everyone you strike a bargain with, you'll settle for my word.''

"Or I'll feel more of the sting a certain Bee carries in her tongue." He stood there for a long minute and then took a step sideways to reach for the front door. "There's more to you than meets the eye, BeeGee. You can turn waspish without warning.''

"Just want to set the record straight," she said as Dan opened the door. "You folks were only passing through, as far as I knew this afternoon. Now I know you'll be buzzing around this hive awhile.''

She might have known he would have to have the last word. Dan smiled at her blinking in the burst of light from the living room. "And I took you for a small worker bee. My mistake, Queen Bee.''

She sat alone after he went in. The muffled sounds inside were animated and happy, inviting her to go and join the fun. But she watched the sky and wondered what kind of deal she had just made. Why did she have this strange premonition that she had got in over her head?

Chapter Three

"Are you sure you don't mind?" Judy was half in, half out the trailer's door. "After a day's work?"

"I wouldn't have volunteered to baby-sit it I wasn't dying to get the socks whipped off me in Chutes and Ladders." BeeGee gestured with her head to where Kip was setting up the board game on the carpet. "You and Alex have ten minutes before the movie starts. Get going while the going's good."

"I really appreciate this," Judy said as Alex dragged her off, still thanking BeeGee. "I can't understand where Dan went...."

"Uncle Dan usually baby-sits me," Kip announced as BeeGee sat down cross-legged next to him. "He lets me win. Will you?"

"Absolutely not, even if I have to cheat." She hunched over the board and rubbed her hands together, making such a ridiculous picture that Kip giggled happily.

BeeGee had stopped by only to see if Judy needed help finding the supermarket. Dinner was on the table and Dan was there, so she had tried to make a fast getaway. but Judy had insisted on giving her coffee and some advice about being a steeplejack. BeeGee knew she needed all the help she could get whenever she contemplated climbing the Cape Coral water tower.

Between the third and fourth cup, Judy had started looking around anxiously for Dan. She and Alex had been planning on an early movie, just the two of them, and her brother-in-law knew it. It wasn't like Dan to wander off without a word, she'd insisted, and he didn't mind baby-sitting whenever he was asked.

"Really?" BeeGee had been rather arch about Dan's disappearance. "Maybe he got a better offer. I could stay for a couple of hours."

Judy wouldn't hear of it. No, Dan would be back in time or they'd make it another night.

"Bring out your cards, Kip, and you can trounce me at Crazy Eights, too, before bedtime," said BeeGee, hanging her head in shame. "I think you loaded these dice. No one can lose four straight games!"

"You and Uncle Dan can," chirped the little boy. "Want to make a snack or bake brownies? Dan does that with me when Mommy and Dad go out."

"He does?" BeeGee couldn't quite visualize Dan in a kitchen or patiently playing with a five-year-old. "Wait a minute. I'll get the door and you deal the cards. No peeking at my hand!"

The doorway was filled up with Dan, who beamed at both of them and thrust an enormous flat cardboard box at BeeGee. "Hi, sport," he said to Kip. "I'm sure my timing's perfect. I hope everyone like mushrooms, black olives and cold pizza. It was a long walk."

"Your timing's lousy," said BeeGee. "You were supposed to be here..."

"And here I am," Dan pointed out. "I knew you wouldn't let Alex and Judy miss their night out. Of course, I checked to make sure they took the Bronco before I scouted for the pizza parlor." He grabbed the box back from BeeGee when she persisted in gaping at him and put it in the microwave oven himself.

"Then you saw my pickup out there and knew I was holding down the fort. To what do we owe the honor of your appearance?" She sat back down with Kip, and reached for her cards.

"Oh, call it curiosity. I just want to know more about our brand-new business partner. We've never worked with anyone outside the family. It's very easy for us to rely on ourselves. We know one another's moves, thoughts, feelings..." Dan came over to them, pizza in hand, and joined the card party.

They started eating and got Kip's cards greasy, and BeeGee did lose the game without being too obvious. With Kip prattling about his new sneakers and his new brother or sister, BeeGee relaxed, admiring Dan's ease and closeness with his nephew.

She didn't even get a chance to put the child to bed. Dan spotted his drooping eyelids and scooped Kip up, whisking him off for a quick change into pajamas and a good-night kiss. Cleaning up the evidence of their fun and games, she debated whether to leave now, without waiting for Alex's and Judy's return.

"I might as well go home," she said as soon as Dan emerged from the bedroom. "You're in charge and you're awfully good with him."

"If I'm in charge, sit down," ordered Dan airily. "I said I was curious about you, and all I've learned so far is that you like kids, pizza and The Incredible Hulk." He stretched out on the couch and indicated a spot next to himself for her. "You stuck around when I showed up. I suspect you're curious about me."

He was right but BeeGee was suddenly eager to leave. Her uneasiness was back, fed by his slightly arrogant attitude toward her. She made an offhand remark about waiting long enough to be sure he wouldn't vanish again and started for the door.

"Please stay," he said unexpectedly. "I didn't take the chance of making Judy mad at me for nothing, I hope. I wanted to talk to you. Somehow, I didn't think if I asked you to go for coffee, you would."

"You make a lot of assumptions," BeeGee replied, without adding that most of them were correct. She wouldn't have gone. "What else do you see in your crystal ball about me?"

She found herself perched on the couch, fascinated almost against her will. Dan had set up this whole evening and it seemed like a lot of trouble to go to. For what? To talk to her about what?

Gossip died hard in small towns. Even a casual inquiry by Dan might very well have yielded some of the old rumors about her. Speculations had risen as soon as BeeGee arrived in Fort Myers. A sixteen-year-old girl who was entirely on her own and didn't say much about her past was fair game for fertile minds. She learned denial didn't kill off lies.

There were still people around who believed what they wanted to believe. The faint whispers that Doc and Emma Alden had taken in not merely a runaway but a teenage tramp, an unwed mother, persisted even after BeeGee stayed put and conducted herself irreproachably. She protected herself by staying slightly aloof and rarely dating, but she couldn't help being edgy and defensive whenever she became the topic of conversation.

But Dan wasn't talking. He was studying her with such intensity that BeeGee was aware of how quiet the room was, how big and overwhelmingly male he was.

"I don't know what I see," he said finally. "You seem so young in a strange way. No just in years. I felt a lot older than twenty-nine when I was talking to you last night on your porch."

She covered her discomfort with a joke. "It's the difference between living in the fast lane and Fort Myers. I don't have much experience with men. You're used to sophisticated ladies."

"Yeah, I had to fight a pack of them off to deliver the pizza tonight," Dan drawled. "That is what you think of me, isn't it? And I'm sizing you up to put another notch in my belt."

"Are you?" BeeGee asked coolly, feeling her stomach swoop alarmingly. "I wouldn't be a very impressive conquest . . . or an easy one."

"No," Dan said with a short chuckle. "I'm testing the waters, I guess. Steeplejacking takes nerve and self-confidence, which you seem to have. It also takes trust in the other guy up there. I think you're afraid of something. Me?"

He sat up straighter and threw his arms across the back of the couch. She had to will herself not to move or look worried.

"Don't be ridiculous," said BeeGee testily. "And don't flatter yourself. I'm not afraid to run my own business, be my own boss and order my own life. And I think you'll see whenever we go to Cape Coral that I'm pretty fearless."

Dan shifted closer to her and smiled. "Wednesday. Is that all right with you?"

Testing. One, two, three, testing, she repeated silently to herself. *He's testing.* "Fine. I don't have anything planned."

His arm came from behind her, brushing her shoulder. He picked up a book from the coffee table and laid it on her lap, touching the top of her bare thigh but removing his hand quickly. "You might be interested in this."

"Not your etchings, is it?" BeeGee flipped through the pages. The entire book was full of newspaper clippings from different states, some with pictures: a Greening scrapbook.

"I just want you to have a good idea of what you signed on for," Dan said softly.

They spent the next half hour poring over the scrapbook and BeeGee asked about a million questions. The more she read about some of the more spectacular jobs they had done, the more unnerved she became. Six-foot ladders were no sweat; sixty-foot towers presented a far different challenge.

One photo, in particular, tickled her. Dan, Alex and Judy dangled under the trestle of a railroad bridge. They were posed as the three famous monkeys who heard, spoke and saw no evil. She started to read the caption.

"The Terrific Trio was clowning around," said Dan, turning the page too quickly.

BeeGee tried to get him to go back to the picture. Laughing made the flicker of fear in her disappear. Nothing was too hard to handle if she could find humor in it. Dan was equally insistent they skip ahead and there was a brief tussle for possession of the scrapbook.

"Don't be silly and let me look. What's wrong? Did they shoot your bad side?" demanded BeeGee.

She was uncommonly strong for a woman but it was no contest. Dan began gently to pry her fingers, one by one, from the edge of the cover until he won. It wasn't unpleasant to hold hands with him and let the warmth of contact creep slowly up her arm.

"I forgot that one was in there. There was a rare foul-up on that bridge. Why study a mistake?" He gave her hand a light squeeze and smiled but there wasn't laughter in his eyes.

"To avoid making the mistake twice," BeeGee replied calmly. "I know there's risk involved. I accept danger better than most folks."

Dan's face came very close to hers. There was the pale stubble of his new beard and a few lines etched into the corners of his eyes but he had no bad side. He was drop-dead attractive and more troubling to her than the prospect of steeplejacking. The wide, sensual sweep of his mouth interested her much more than the book he was clutching.

"You'll be as safe as in a cradle," Dan contradicted her. "We do things right. You don't have a thing to worry about."

She felt slightly muddled as if they were talking about two different subjects. It wasn't what he said; it was the low, soothing way he said it. He looked more into her than at her and the piercing power hit some well-hidden nerve. She was sure Dan was going to make a pass at her and the feeling gathering inside told her she wasn't contemplating leaping off the couch.

"But you're on the right track about not making the same mistake," he said suddenly, and flipped open to the page in question. He jabbed a finger at the photo, drawing her attention to a thick white band on Alex's ankle. "He fractured it and went right back up to finish the bridge."

Reading the short account of the accident made the fog in her brain lift. Alex was quoted as saying it was his own fault. He had rigged without allowing for the damp weather, the slippage and stretching of wet ropes. She made up her mind to be careful. She asked about the pose, ready to move on to more successful ventures.

"Even monkeys fall out of trees," kidded Dan. "It helps if you're slightly bananas to begin with in this line of work."

He liked to hear her laugh, a surprisingly full sound for such a small woman. She didn't giggle; she smiled a lot but it was hard to get her to unleash the laughter. While BeeGee bent her dark head over the scrapbook once more, he studied her.

He amazed himself. There wouldn't have been much of a protest if he'd moved in a minute ago, taken her in his arms and found out what BeeGee Chambers tasted like, felt like. The moment had come and gone and he hadn't seized it or her. He wasn't sure why.

His unusual reluctance wasn't for lack of interest. In a compact, scaled-down way she was lovely. She actually tried to play her looks down. The lack of any makeup fooled him into thinking she was younger but whenever BeeGee glanced up at him, her eyes were impossibly fringed with black lace, her delicately sculpted mouth a rosy invitation.

BeeGee reached down and scratched a mosquito bite on her bare ankle. He contemplated her legs and cleared his throat. It was a crime to cover up those smoothly tanned and perfectly proportioned legs in jeans. Of course, when she walked toward him on the couch tonight, he was aware of some distinctly criminal thoughts. But he wasn't going to act on them.

Too young? Too innocent? No, there was a wariness in her every look and an undercurrent of maturity beyond her years in some of the things she said. She knew exactly what he was thinking when he talked about doing things right.

If he wasn't sitting there idly for lack of interest, the possibility of too much interest developing loomed up for Dan. Absolutely not, he thought with a trace of anger. The idea made him get up hastily and refill their stoneware mugs with fresh coffee, distancing himself from the floral scent of her freshly shampooed hair and the heat of her body right next to him.

"You should feel honored," he said to BeeGee, bringing back the cups. "I broke a cardinal rule asking you to join the crew. It wasn't just the insurance problem. After seeing the clippings, you known what kind of team dependency this takes."

"Are you backing out?" Her voice held the no-nonsense inflection Dan was beginning to recognize. "Well, I'm not. Tonight convinced me to go for it. You can't psych me out, Dan."

He put the mug into her hand. "You get your feathers ruffled easily. I was telling you what's what, not backing out of the deal. When the situation changes, some rules are meant to be broken. I'm convinced meeting you yesterday was more than a coincidence. You're just about perfect ... for this job.''

"For one thing, I have my own insurance,'' she said dryly. "I'm also goofy or greedy enough to want to do it.''

"Both,'' judged Dan. "My brother and Judy were sold on including you as soon as I pointed out the rarity of finding a crazy, ambitious lady on a ladder.''

"I'm honored.''

They were laughing when the handle rattled and the front door opened.

"Well, looky here,'' said Judy. She nudged Alex in the ribs. "Dan must be showing off for you, BeeGee. He hardly ever looks at that old mess of paper. Did he and Kippy behave?''

"Good as gold,'' BeeGee said. "Hope you enjoyed the movie.''

Judy nodded but she also yawned.

BeeGee took it as a hint and made her exit. She had a full day looming ahead of her but sleep eluded her. She kept thinking ahead to Wednesday and wondering what awaited her. Her dreams, when sleep finally came, were strange. She saw herself climbing up the prow of a Viking ship, and at the top of the elaborately carved dragon figurehead, a tall blond man was laughing and holding his hand out to her. The ship rocked violently and she plummeted headlong into darkness.

Chapter Four

She didn't see the Greenings—any of them—again until the day they had agreed on. More precisely, the dawn of the day. BeeGee stood draped sleepily over the mailbox waiting for Dan and Alex.

"You're not exactly bright eyed and bushy tailed," Dan said as he got out of the Bronco. "Having second thoughts?"

She was wedged in between the two brothers. "I'm still getting my first thoughts together," BeeGee admitted. "I'm a morning person but this is too early!"

Half the job was in the rigging, explained Alex as they drove along and the higher the climb, the more time it took to make the tackle secure. He always tested every rope, ladder rung and pulley.

BeeGee rubbed her eyes, nodded and swallowed a yawn.

"There it is," said Dan, waving his hand out the open window to the tower. "And we do have an audience, small but ready to be thrilled and chilled."

There were a few people meandering around the base of the water tower or sitting in cars. BeeGee wondered why anyone sane would wake at this hour to see someone else paint. She didn't attract a crowd very often when she was putting up a new TV antenna.

"Hey, there, BeeGee," called a male voice. "Moving up in the world?" The bystander convulsed himself with his wit.

She didn't respond once she saw it was a former high-school classmate. His name escaped her but not the memory of a dance where she'd had to trounce solidly on his instep to remind him she wasn't a book written in Braille.

Alex and Dan were already at work. She wasn't required to do anything but admire their efficiency and gracefulness as they set up the job. There was a good deal to admire but her ability to appreciate competency was somewhat diminished that morning.

The water tower must have grown since she'd last taken a look at it. It was monstrous, a globe set on four unscalable legs. An enormous ladder enabled Alex to reach the series of tiny metal handgrips and he scampered effortlessly upward. There was even a smattering of applause from the onlookers when he reached the slightly flattened spot at the very top of the huge metal storage tank. Heavy cables, thicker than her wrist, would hold up their tackle.

Safe as a cradle. BeeGee walked closer and the nearer she drew to it, the taller the tower became. Or was she shrinking? How lucky she hadn't taken the time for breakfast. There would never have been enough room for the arriving swarm of butterflies *and* breakfast in her stomach.

"Safe as a cradle?" she said to Dan. "Do you, by any chance, remember the Rock-a-bye rhyme? 'And down will come baby, cradle and all.'"

BeeGee picked up one of the boatswain chairs for her own inspection. It was a piece of wood to sit on, held in the center of a web of ropes; it didn't fill her with confidence. There was a canvas-and-metal safety belt as if falling out was more a problem than falling straight down.

She shaded her eyes with one hand and craned her neck to get the full picture of what she had agreed to. *Not a chance,* she thought. *Feet, do your stuff and let's walk home.*

"Alex has got the rigging secured," announced Dan. His voice was notably soft in her ear and BeeGee could almost feel his body as he stepped right up behind her. "Piece of cake, really. With the three of us, it'll be done in no time."

Alex looked like an ant on an apple at the top of the tower. He waved at them and shouted down, lowering himself slightly to his starting point.

"Ready? Scared?" Dan seemed to know the answer. He linked his fingers with BeeGee's and started forward.

Her knees bent and her feet did move, to her surprise. Her fingers were icy but securely wrapped in his warm ones. Step by reluctant step, she was taking up the challenge, trying to persuade herself that nervousness was first cousin to excitement, not a heart attack.

"We were all afraid in the beginning," Dan was saying conversationally, the way someone else would tell her he went to a movie. "Once you get into it, it's so much fun you have to remind yourself every once in a while that it *is* dangerous, so you don't get tempted to take stupid chances."

"Sort of like falling in love," BeeGee heard herself reply in a tight, too high voice.

Dan stopped helping her into the chair and let the two safety-belt straps slip from his hands. Instead, he cupped her face and tilted it up toward his, making her wide brown eyes meet his calm blue ones, studying the cheeks she knew were flushed, the lips she felt go bloodless and numb.

His own mouth twitched suspiciously, not quite breaking into a smile. "You'll do just fine, BeeGee. Now, one last thing...old family ritual for luck."

There *was* feeling in her lips. The second Dan's mouth descended onto hers, a whole world of feeling returned. Her heart suddenly remembered it was supposed to pump and warmth shot through her, thawing the ice in finger and toes. Fear melted fast under the pressure of his kiss. The heaviness in her dissolved magically, and if Dan wasn't cradling her face she might have floated up.

When his tongue skimmed over her dry lower lip, BeeGee could only think of that sweet, damp touch, the feel of his breath mingled with hers. His body blocked the sight of the tower. She was soft, pliant and so willing....

"And now to work," murmured Dan, taking his mouth away from hers slowly. "Tell me that BeeGee can do it. Tell me you aren't worried."

"BeeGee can do it," she recited dutifully. And she wasn't worried about scaling the Eiffel Tower in a high wind. Anything would be a snap if she got a kiss for luck from Dan. That was her worry!

She didn't have a bit of trouble following him up to where Alex was working. It was simple to match her movements to his, doing whatever he did and keeping her features composed, looking around as the trees and people shrank under their feet and the Bronco grew smaller. Now if only she could be as matter-of-fact about a kiss and the way he'd made her feel, there would be no worry at all.

Alex and Dan worked fast, much faster than she did. They shouted and chatted back and forth, cracking jokes and taking short breaks to marvel at the beauty of the area surrounding them. After a while, BeeGee relaxed enough to join in.

It wasn't scary. It was a completely new perspective on her familiar world; she could pick out houses and buildings she knew, look over at the crisscrossed causeways and see tiny boats she recognized. Greens and blues were especially vivid, bathed in sunshine. Everything had a postcard perfection to it and it was surprisingly quiet. A bird flew by, close enough to reach out and touch.

She found herself gazing off dreamily, caught up in light flashing on water, brilliant white crescents of beaches, a kiss that shouldn't mean anything. With real effort she concentrated on her section and finished it, lowering herself slowly to a new spot.

"See? I told you it was a little like flying. You're almost an angel up here." Dan's voice broke into her consciousness. "You can't live on clouds as a steady diet, though. Alex is heading down for lunch. You want to join him or grab lunch and a break up here with me?"

BeeGee pulled out her wristwatch, pinned in her work-shirt's breast pocket. The hours had gone by like minutes. It didn't seem possible she had spent four hours in this crazy swinglike contraption.

"How are we going to get lunch? Bird delivery?" She grinned and scratched at her peeling nose.

The mention of food and the prospect of a cold drink made her stomach rumble. Alex obliged by sending up a carton on the rope packed with sandwiches and a fresh thermos of iced tea. Dan held out one offering after another, affecting a terrible French accent.

"Perhaps mademoiselle cares for the superb ham-and-cheese...the subtle but exquisite peanut-butter-and-jelly, a great favorite of *le petit* Kip." He filled the top of the thermos bottle with tea and sipped at it. "Ah, a fine vintage . . . a magnificent year, Tuesday."

BeeGee laughed and reached for the cup. "You're crazy. Or you need a bigger hat. I think the sun has fried your brain."

"Fried brains? No, I'm sorry *ma belle*, they are not on the menu today."

Even a simple snack at sixty-five feet was different. No sandwich ever tasted better, no tea was colder or more refreshing, no sidewalk café in Paris offered a better view. They braced themselves with their feet, leaning back and out, and behaved as if they were on a picnic.

"Is it always this much fun?" marveled BeeGee. "All we need is a red-checked tablecloth and some music."

"I could whistle," offered Dan. "Let's see, 'Over the Rainbow,' 'High and the Mighty'? Name your tune." He edged closer and took the cup they were passing back and forth, making his fingers cover BeeGee's but not allowing her to let go. "As for fun, the answer is no. Having you here sent my enjoyment quotient over the top."

"Thanks," BeeGee said quietly. The shaky feeling was back and she couldn't blame it on the height. A simple kiss, a lingering touch, a certain look from this man and she was tempted to take stupid chances.

The longer Dan stayed around and the more she saw of him, the easier it would be to forget herself and tell him too much. From past experience, BeeGee knew what a mistake telling the truth could be. Finding the right man to confide in was some silly, adolescent, romantic dream, she supposed. Whenever she'd told a man about herself before, it had been like posting a notice. Open season on BeeGee Chambers.

Lulled by the warmth and interest of Dan's blue eyes, she imagined what would happen if she explained how she ended up in Fort Myers. It would be a relief to be open and talk freely about the aimless, scary years. Dan might understand and believe she had survived virtually untouched but not unscathed. She had seen the worst in her travels, and her few brushes with men had been creepy, narrow escapes. Suspicions lingered and it was smarter and safer to stay everyone's buddy, nobody's woman.

Dan had already given her a gift he might not be aware of. He was the first man she had ever wanted as a woman. Desire was a natural and good feeling; it made BeeGee happy just to know the past hadn't blunted her needs or made her bitter.

Wait, her careful nature warned. *The right man is bound to understand you and make you want him. He'll stay around for a long, long time.* Dan was going, no matter what she said or did. Daydreaming did not change the reality. BeeGee felt slightly sick to her stomach.

"Maybe you ought to call time-out," Dan said. A frown appeared, drawing his eyebrows closer together and creasing a V above his nose. "Go and stretch your legs, make a pit stop if you like. You went a shade pale there."

"The air's too thin," she feebly joked. "Not enough oxygen to my brain while I digest."

He was concerned but annoyance also crept into his voice. "Okay, BeeGee, I forgot. You're your own boss. Nobody tells you what to do. I accept the fact that you do a man's job. I just keep remembering that you're a woman. My problem, right?"

"Right," she snapped back. *And mine,* she added mentally. Let him think the issue was tomboy pride or women's lib or whatever he liked. The problem was Dan and how close she'd come to making a fool of herself because of him.

The tower's shadow was beginning to stretch out across the ground before Alex called a halt. Most of the work was done and Alex was in high spirits. He didn't appear to notice that BeeGee had been exceptionally quiet, during the afternoon, concentrating on her painting.

"This was terrific! A great idea to recruit BeeGee, Dan, and a good day's work; Judy's liable to be ticked off when she realizes it went almost as smoothly as it would have if she'd been up there with us...."

Alex went on and on, his enthusiasm and the radio filling up the Bronco with cheerful noise. BeeGee got a playful tap on her arm and lots of compliments. Dan stared silently out the window, unwilling or unable to echo his older brother's sentiments.

They made one stop on the way to the trailer park. Alex had insisted on finding a supermarket and darted out of the truck, leaving BeeGee and Dan to sit with the motor running.

"He's going to get Judy something," Dan said, although no explanation had been offered by Alex. "He does that. It may be flowers but more likely it will be a weird ice-cream flavor... pistachio-peach-ripple."

"You mean Judy *is* going to be angry or feel slighted?" BeeGee was upset at the very idea. She started to tell Dan that Judy was so nice, so jolly about the prospect of being replaced. She would never have considered steeplejacking, she went on, even if it paid off all her bills in full, if Judy was going to feel usurped by a newcomer, a novice, and—

"Whoa," ordered Dan, half turning in the seat. He put his hand firmly over BeeGee's mouth, draping his other arm around her and holding her steady. "Would you stop jumping to conclusions at every opportunity? Don't try to talk. Just nod your head for yes."

Her dark curls bobbed in assent. She didn't like being muzzled and scolded like a naughty child but couldn't help noticing how good it felt to be held by him. There was the pressure of his chest against her arm, crushing the small curve of her breast almost flat. There was the meeting of thighs. BeeGee was very much aware of the hardness and strength of muscle, the length of his legs.

"You are the most exasperating, suspicious and, I might add, mysterious female I have ever..." He stopped when she glared at him. "All right, no lecture, but listen. I'll make it very, very simple. I wanted you to work with us. Judy liked the idea. She did not and does not and will not hate it when she finds out you were a roaring success. She and Alex want this baby too much for her to take any chances. Am I getting through?"

Another nod was all she was allowed. BeeGee tried to pull away his hand, wriggling and pushing on him. The only thing she accomplished by rubbing against him that way was waking up a lot of nerve endings in her body. Anger and frustration at being manhandled—and so easily—must have showed. She desperately hoped that her excitement was not as readable.

"When I want you to talk, you clam up. When I won't let you talk, you practically burn holes in me with those big eyes," continued Dan, but he was speaking in a sweeter, almost pleading tone. "Now, Alex went to buy Judy a present, but not to make up for anything anyone has done. He is constantly giving her some silly little thing or slipping a note in her lunch. She does it, too. That's called love, BeeGee, and even some old married folks are guilty of it."

She saw Alex making his way back to them. She briefly debated biting the callused palm over her mouth and rejected that idea. A few muffled, frantic sounds and wild signaling with her eyes alerted Dan to take his hand back.

"You've got some kind of chip on your shoulder," finished Dan quickly before Alex got there. "You take offense when there's none offered and I'd like to know why."

Alex deposited the brown paper sack on BeeGee's lap and stuck a lollipop under her nose. "For you, dear lady, with my admiration. It's root beer. They didn't have orange. Imagine, Florida and they are out of orange. No, don't thank me, please. It's a mere token.''

"You're too kind," BeeGee said a trifle hoarsely. The Greenings were strange people in a lot of ways. They made her feel comfortable and awkward with them almost at the same time. She had been in this unfamiliar emotional jumble since the day she saw them and it was getting worse, not better. She unwrapped the gift and popped it into her mouth, avoiding the need to say anything more.

When the old BeeGee was puzzled by people, frightened or confused, she ran away. The new BeeGee found herself staying after dinner, sitting across the kitchen table from Judy and studying the gold flecks in the tabletop. She sipped a cup of strong black coffee.

"Are you positive you don't want to try this fudge-pecan-praline? It sounds as though you burned your calories working, and skinny as you are, it won't leave any unsightly lumps." Judy smiled and patted her stomach with satisfaction. "I have an excuse and I'll use it with every gallon I lap up."

"The tower wasn't as bad as I dreaded," admitted BeeGee. "Actually, I really liked doing the job. Alex and Dan were determined to make me feel I could hack it and that I was one of you steeplejacks. It was exactly as if you were there—old family ritual and all. Well, I guess it works because I went up. And it is a novel way to start every job."

"Old family ritual?" repeated Judy. "The ice cream, you mean. No, ice cream comes after."

BeeGee gave up playing Connect the Dots with her fingernail, and her head slowly rose. "The kiss, of course. The kiss for luck."

"Alex kissed you?" Judy made a face of mock horror. "That dirty dog! He always is up there rigging us and I'm content with a wave and a whistle. Show him a pretty young thing and he kisses her."·

BeeGee started to explain and Judy's expression changed dramatically. She struggled so hard to keep her mirth under control and failed so miserably that BeeGee didn't have to be told.

"There is no such tradition," BeeGee said sheepishly. "Dan made it up because I was paralyzed with fear and he thought I was going to back out."

"Well, there is a tradition now," retorted Judy. She laughed until she had to pat the corners of her eyes with a crumpled paper napkin. "What a sneak my brother-in-law is! I can't believe Dan had to resort to such tactics to get a kiss. He doesn't usually strike out with women using the direct approach."

"I'm sure he doesn't," BeeGee said tensely. "I'll bet this is going to be worth some teasing if I agree to do that steeple they talked about."

Judy smiled and licked her spoon. Her face lit up with a mischievous look. "I'm not so sure you were the butt of a joke or a coward to be coaxed. I wonder if Dan just caught a glimpse of the highest tower."

"Huh? What's that?"

Judy shook her head and collected the dishes and mugs to wash. "Don't ask me. My lips are sealed. One of these days, real soon, ask Dan about the highest tower. Only don't ask him when you're up in the air."

"Why not?" BeeGee wanted to know.

Judy looked over her shoulder from the sink and gave BeeGee a long, measuring appraisal. "'Cause then he'll already have his hands full and you'd miss the finer points of his explanation." She whipped the suds into a froth, laughing to herself, and stoutly refused to say another word.

Their gabfest ended abruptly. Alex and Dan came in with a plea to venture outside and play volleyball. BeeGee begged off, claiming this day was the second most exhausting one of her life. She couldn't remember one that topped it but there *must* have been one. She wasn't tired, however. A kind of nervous energy was coursing through her, the residual excitement of her day's experiences.

"I'll walk home slowly," she said, "and hope this feeling wears off."

"I'll drive you...or walk with you. It's dark," Dan offered immediately.

Behind his back, Judy made a peak with both her hands and mouthed, "Ask him." BeeGee shook her head no to both of them. Whatever the highest tower was, it could wait and she was in no shape to climb it. If Dan went with her, the peculiar feeling might well get worse; he was, in part, personally responsible for getting her this wound up.

Dan was not acquainted with the word *no*, she suspected. He caught up to her before she got half a block from the trailer park, falling right into step with her and not even breathing hard. She didn't want to talk but her reticence didn't slow him down. Dan wanted to know which stadium they were passing, who played there, what the streets and parks were named after—in short, everything.

"The Kansas City Royals use it for spring training. And that's Tecumseh Park over there, fireworks on Fourth of July," BeeGee replied dutifully, keeping her travelogue to a minimum. Dan walked so close his body kept brushing against hers. From time to time he made a point of taking her elbow or touching her arm to get her attention when she lapsed in muteness.

"Are you mad about something?" he asked finally.

BeeGee suppressed her urge to laugh. "Not anymore. I was peeved when I found out the truth about an old family ritual that doesn't exist. But it doesn't matter. It won't happen again."

"Okay, it won't," he said. "Next time, I'll ask."

Next time? He sounded so sure there would be a next time. BeeGee wasn't even sure she had taken the right shortcut. She was too absorbed in the strange way she felt just being with him, the strange thoughts he evoked. The familiar path home was like an exotic journey to an unknown destination. There were huge white trumpet-shaped flowers opening to the lure of moonlight, scenting the air. The chorus of frogs from inside the park sounded fuller and richer when she and

Dan stopped for a minute to listen than it did when she heard it from the porch.

Their steps seemed to get shorter and shorter. Fewer words passed between them as they got near the house and clinic.

"Well, thanks for keeping me company," BeeGee said awkwardly. "I could give you coffee before my coma sets in...."

"You could give me a kiss good-night," Dan suggested. "You see, I asked." He stood there motionless, waiting.

BeeGee turned to him. She wanted to see his face but it was shadowed. "Yes," she said a little tentatively, expecting to feel his arms move around, his mouth to come closer. Nothing happened.

It took her a few seconds of looking up at Dan, who towered a full foot over her, to realize what he had asked. She was giving him a kiss, not having one taken from her. His direct approach made her feel both bold and shy at the same time.

BeeGee climbed up one step. It took two steps to get level with him. She backed up the second step and rested her hands on his shoulders. Even prepared by what had happened this morning, the surge of wonder at the kiss's brief contact still amazed her. Didn't Dan feel it, too? Didn't one kiss lead to another?

"My turn," he said as if she had spoken. "Is that all right?"

It was more than all right. It was a fine idea. She managed to nod once, not wanting to rely on a voice she was sure would squeak.

His hands reached as if to enfold her and then he hesitated, drawing them down along both her arms in a stroke as light as the caress of the night wind. His lips pressed hers in a kiss more fleeting and chaste than the one she had given him, only a shadow of what she thought it would be.

"Good night, BeeGee," Dan whispered, merging with the darkness and disappearing in a few steps. "Thanks, partner."

Finishing her sidewalk patch and losing the patio order were not the end of the world. There were other jobs around. She'd have to get busy the next day and find them. The healthy deposit from her share of the water-tower adventure would keep her going, but not forever.

A horn blared and she jumped back onto the curb, heart beating wildly. "Watch where you're going, you... Oh, it's you," she stammered as the Bronco screeched to a stop.

"Watch where you're going, yourself," Dan laughed. "I must have covered fifty miles looking for you. Want a cold drink?"

BeeGee hesitated only a minute. Even if he was exaggerating, Dan was plainly delighted to catch up with her. It was almost scary to hear her own laughter bubble and catch in her throat, triggered by the mere sight of him. The day felt as if it was starting all over.

"Sure. Why not?" She got in, telling him about the work she'd done and asking about Judy. "This week was good for her. She looked great last night."

"The week was good for all of us," Dan said. "I was hunting you down to tell you that and a few other things." He pulled in the parking lot of the hamburger joint and leaned across to open BeeGee's door.

For a second, when his arm touched her in passing and his body was inclined sharply toward her, she thought he was going to kiss her. There was an exuberant air about Dan today, infectious and real. BeeGee moved to meet the kiss and bumped heads with him.

"Sorry," he said with a surprised look. "Are you always in a hurry?"

"Only lately," she grumbled, rubbing her forehead and sliding out.

"My treat," Dan declared once they were inside, paying for a soft drink for her and three hamburgers for himself. "Just call me sugar daddy."

"Last of the big-time spenders." laughed BeeGee as they sat down. "You are in a good mood! What happened?"

"We lost the Tallahassee job," Dan said between bites.

"I lost my patio job and I'm not exactly whooping it up."

"Aw, listen, will you?" He held up his hand, threatening to muzzle her, and smiled. "Tallahassee is a long haul and none of us is anxious to leave right away. Don't you like having us around?"

Too much, she thought. She took a long sip of her drink, contenting herself with a nod. Yes, she liked them around.

"I thought so. And you got a kick out of working with us, too. After the initial terror, I mean." He licked catsup from his thumb and winked at her. "How about another crack at steeplejacking?"

Disappointment made the drink taste sour. Aloud, she asked what he was talking about, which job. Silently, BeeGee chided herself for being a fool, a dolt and a dreamer. What was she thinking? A daydream scenario where the Greenings settled down in Fort Myers and everyone lived happily ever after? No, this was business. Strictly business and very temporary.

"I drove out with Alex and this steeple is an easy job," Dan was saying. "A quaint, old clapboard church—"

"I know it," BeeGee broke in. "The place looks haunted, right?"

"Yes. Well, will you do it? A belfry repair should make you a full-fledged steeplejack."

She pictured the old church in her mind. It didn't seem like a death-defying day's work. "Okay," she agreed without much enthusiasm. "I'll make sure there's nothing scheduled for Friday."

"That's my girl!" Dan crumpled up the wrappers and stood up to throw them away. He bent down suddenly and touched his lips to BeeGee's cheek.

She was not his girl. The spot where he had kissed her cheek tickled but she wouldn't reach up and touch it. All she could do when he came back to the table was watch the movement of his wide, chiseled mouth and wonder what it would be like to be kissed as if he

meant it. No family ritual, no sealing a bargain between them, no good-night.

When Dan had to repeat his question a third time,
BeeGee realized she was staring, not listening. She
concentrated on his hands, but that was no better. For
a man, he had beautiful hands. Strong, large but well-
shaped. The light in the restaurant glinted off blond
hair on his wrists.

"I said, Judy invited you for dinner tonight. But
Alex is the cook. Forewarned is forearmed." Dan
reached across the laminated table and pinched her
nose. "Hello, anybody home?"

"No," admitted BeeGee with a sigh. "My brain is
out to lunch. I'll brave Alex's culinary skills. I'm
fearless."

She was reminded of something Judy had said. Dan
did not have his hands full and they weren't dangling
from ropes now.

"What's the highest tower?" BeeGee asked. "It
sounds like a riddle but . . ." She forgot what she was
going to say. Dan's expression turned murderous.

"Who's the blabbermouth? Judy or my brother?
The highest tower, huh?" He took their paper cups
and chucked them into the trash can.

"I wasn't done with my drink," BeeGee said angrily. "Sorry I asked. I didn't mean to pry."

"Love is the highest tower." Dan bit off each word.
"Let's go."

Without waiting, he was out of the restaurant and
stalking to the truck. BeeGee hurried after him, totally bewildered at his reaction. He was usually so

cool, so controlled. Why love—or the mere mention of it—would bend him out of shape mystified her.

"She told me to mention it. Judy." BeeGee slammed her door hard and turned to glare at Dan. He was slumped behind the wheel, tapping his forefinger on his chin. "Said you had a glimpse of it or something like that. Never mind!"

"I do mind," he said in a more subdued voice. "Kind of a private family joke. The highest tower is love and once you scale it, you can't get down. You can't even fall off if it's really love. You just stay there, at the very pinnacle."

An inflection in Dan's words, an odd look on his face warned BeeGee not to push farther. But nothing could stop the speculations that rose in her. He didn't sound happy. If she didn't know better, she would have said he sounded lonely and bitter.

She picked at the patch on her knee and wished she could recall exactly the conversation with Judy. It was possible Dan had been in love once and couldn't get over it. Maybe he hadn't loved anyone since, because he was stranded on an emotional peak long ago and faraway.

"You make love sound awful," BeeGee muttered, glancing over at him. She didn't expect a reply. He seemed miles away. She wasn't prepared for his eyes to focus on her suddenly with a determined, decidedly cool look.

"Not as awful as it was," Dan said flatly. "The jokes about the bride being jilted at the altar haven't struck me as funny since we left Michigan. Technically, I guess, I was the one who went away but that's not how it was supposed to be. I wasn't going alone.''

There were times that being right brought no satisfaction. This was one of those times. BeeGee repeated her apology and once again assured him she had never intended to pry into his private life. The remnant of pain she glimpsed in his eyes was more than enough for her. The undercurrent of regret in his voice made her want to back off this whole subject.

"She was all for marriage and moving...at first," Dan said, as if BeeGee hadn't spoken. "To a rich girl, it must have sounded like running away to join the circus or going off to sea. Two brothers and their wives on the road for the grand tour, that sort of thing. But then, when she realized it wasn't going to be an extended honeymoon but for life..."

"She" didn't even have a name but BeeGee began to form a picture of her as he talked. He has been engaged to a wealthy, sleek blonde for a year before he left his real-estate investments. She must have been gorgeous, willowy, tall, thought BeeGee miserably. The woman had driven a spike deep into Dan's heart four years earlier when she'd called off their wedding.

"Well, we both got what we wanted...or deserved," finished Dan. "She's married to a mortgage banker in her father's firm, a real climber in another sense."

Love was a mistake Dan didn't intend to make twice. BeeGee understood the unspoken message. She should be grateful for his candid reminder that theirs was a business relationship and nothing more. Judy deserved her thanks, too. If BeeGee hadn't mentioned the highest tower, she might go on fantasizing about Dan's interest in her.

"About that dinner tonight..." BeeGee began when the silence in the truck became noticeable. "I better take a rain check on it." She paused, trying to come up with a plausible excuse for her sudden change of plans and failing.

"Okay," Dan said without any argument. He backed out of the parking lot and headed back to BeeGee's pickup, driving faster than necessary. "I'll tell Alex the church is on for Friday."

"You might want to slow down before we reach the speed of light," commented BeeGee. "Friday will get here soon enough. No need to go through the time warp."

There was no response from Dan. BeeGee was puzzled by the strained expression his face and this minor show of recklessness.

"Let me out here," she demanded. "I'd rather walk a few blocks. With old what's-her-name on your brain, you're in a dangerous frame of mind."

"Diane," growled Dan. He did, however, ease his foot off the accelerator. "I'd rather talk about something else."

BeeGee glanced in the mirror on her side. "Try sweet talk," she suggested.

"Would you be receptive right now?" asked Dan.

"Not me, but you may want to see how far it goes on the man following us," said BeeGee with a smile.

Dan caught sight of the police car trailing them, blue light flashing. "People are always saying that love hurts. It costs, too. Five dollars for every mile over the speed limit."

"You'd know that was cheap if you'd ever been in love," Dan shot back as he pulled over. He raised himself slightly off the seat and eased his wallet out of his hip pocket. "But you haven't and it shows, BeeGee. I hope...well, I hope you find the climb easier and less costly."

The policeman made a production of checking the out-of-state license plates and reading every line of Dan's license. Once he recognized BeeGee in the passenger seat, he relaxed his ramrod posture visibly and decided a verbal scolding and a final "Take it slow and easy" sufficed.

BeeGee couldn't resist a small dig. "You got off scot-free, Dan," she said as she hopped out around the corner. "From getting a ticket, anyway."

"I hope so," he replied cryptically, "but maybe you ought to check with Judy. She thinks she knows more about me than I do."

Chapter Five

The First Baptist Church was undoubtedly pictur-esque. It was stuck all by itself on a side road just out of town. No matter how often the building was painted white, the old wood quickly resumed a soft silvery-gray color. The once gold cross at the steeple's top listed slightly to one side, marking the passage of a particularly severe storm. The steeple's slatted sides were marred by many cracked or missing wooden louvers.

"Straighten the cross and secure. Replace and re-pair slats," read Alex to them. "That's what we con-tracted for, but—" he produced a small can of expensive gilding paint "—I think we'll throw in a touch-up for nothing. Do good works and leave our mark behind us."

BeeGee ceased struggling with a heavy pulley and let Dan and Alex unload and assemble the others. "You're a gentleman," she praised. "This isn't very big or rich."

"I'd spring for a genuine releafing of the gold, if I could," Alex remarked. He set up a ladder to reach the roof and got busy rigging lines to the tall boxed structure of the belfry.

BeeGee watched avidly and without apprehension. The steeple was nowhere near as high as the water tower. She was surprised to feel a real eagerness to start. Dan had said every job was different and she believed him now, watching Alex and Dan figure out the best approach and carefully testing the ropes.

"Whew, there's a bad whiff of something up there today," complained Alex when he came down. "Is there a factory around here? A processing plant?"

"Not out here," said BeeGee. She glanced over at Dan. He had been unusually quiet on the ride over and preoccupied while Alex was working. Dan took out his baseball cap and nervously adjusted it several times. "We're on, King Kong! Are you planning to stand and squint at the sun all morning?"

"See anything unusual?" Dan ignored her.

"Yeah, a job for two, not three," smirked Alex. "I'll be the ground crew. If you need help, holler." He indicated a shady spot nearby where he could be found.

"Rats," BeeGee exclaimed succinctly, peeved at Dan's peculiar behavior and Alex's devil-may-care attitude. She went over to the ladder to make the climb and was elbowed aside by Dan.

"Age before beauty," he insisted from the third rung.

"Pearls before swine," she grumbled up at him, "and the runt always comes last. I can do it!"

He swung his leg over the pitch of the roof and waited for her, offering his hand as she joined him. "Never a doubt, BeeGee. I'd just as soon double-check."

She was already snapping herself into the safety belt and eyeing the distance to the top. His hand touched her forearm in a light but restraining way and she turned her head. The fleeting thought of the old family ritual came to mind but Dan only muttered something about going first.

Without bothering to argue, BeeGee began to haul herself upward, keeping her gaze sensibly on the steeple and not on Dan. She had never liked being bossed around, and the younger Mr. Greening had a tinge of the overbearing male, she decided silently. He was used to telling women what to do and getting his way.

There was a funny, not very pleasant smell as she went up higher. She made a face and held her nose, peering down at Dan a few feet below and to the left of her.

"You stick out your tongue at me and I'll paddle your rear end," Dan said. "I only wanted to be sure that—"

She found out what he wanted to be sure of at that very second. There was a rustling noise above her and a dark shape whizzed over her head. More scratching, rustling and movement alerted her. From between the louvers a horde of disturbed and disgruntled bats poured out into the sky, inches from her.

BeeGee slumped down in the bosun's chair, making herself as tiny a target as possible, and cowered. The noise of their wings sweeping by was bad enough but there was also a hideous piercing shrill sound. She wasn't entirely sure whether it was coming from the exiting swarm or from inside her throat.

Dan tried to signal her and to shout instructions but she was not in the mood to listen. Every time there was the slightest contact, the hair-ruffling sensation of a near miss, she flailed her hands wildly to keep the bats as far away as possible. In a matter of minutes, hordes of the nasty creatures had emerged from the belfry.

"Start down," ordered Dan loudly. "Down...right now." He gestured with his thumb and shouted until BeeGee was forced to nod an acknowledgment and make herself go through the motions.

Once she was sliding slowly down the face of the building, it was possible to look up. The bats were high above, wheeling around and moving off en masse. The initial paralyzing fear subsided a bit, but her heart was pounding so violently BeeGee was sure it could pop the buttons off the front of her blue chambray shirt. Reality was almost manageable from this distance and she expected her momentary panic would inspire a laugh or two from Dan and Alex.

She braced herself ten or twelve feet from the ground and glanced over, waving feebly at Dan to stop, too. Her mouth opened and her brain assembled the words. She was ready to suggest they ought to go ahead and finish what they'd started. Nothing came out. She was more shaken than she'd thought and Dan insisted once more, almost angrily, that she keep going.

"Yech!" BeeGee summed it up, finding her voice the second her toes touched the pavement. "Oh, yech-h-h."

"What a mess of them," shouted Alex happily from his position on the truck's tailgate. He was too absorbed in watching the bats to leave his post. "Boy, oh, boy, when they started out, I remembered that time I crawled into a belfry with a beehive inside—"

"Shut up," snapped Dan, too far away to be heard. He called BeeGee's name until she glanced over, wide-eyed and still panting slightly. "Are you okay?"

She wasn't sure. He was pale under his tan but BeeGee imagined she was probably a pastel green from the anxious way he was looking at her. A noncommittal "um-um" didn't satisfy him.

"Stand up and come here," he instructed. "Let me check and make sure you didn't get bitten."

"I'm fine," she answered, an obvious lie that didn't fool him, either. Dan ducked out of the rigging and started over to her. BeeGee didn't trust her legs to hold her up and stayed put. A few stragglers were still leaving the steeple and she hung limply on the ropes and concentrated on them.

Dan's hands, not hers, undid her safety belt and Dan's hands yanked her up onto her feet. His fingers brushed impatiently through the dark mass of curls around her face and touched a smudge on her cheek very gently.

"Just dirt," he sighed with relief. "There's a scratch or two here on your neck. You probably did that, flapping your hands around...."

It was very nice to feel the lingering warmth of his fingers on the side of her throat. It was very, very nice to have Dan so close she couldn't see anything else but him. She couldn't recall the stench of bats that had made her wince because Dan smelled so good and clean.

"Well, I'm all right," amended BeeGee. It didn't sound as steady as she would have liked but it wasn't necessarily because she was scared. "None of the bats bit me. None of them is stuck in my hair."

A faint smile was meant to reassure him. Dan stepped even closer and gripped both her shoulders hard.

"Good," he said thickly. "I got frightened witless but you're fine, huh? You're pretty tough.... You're..."

Alex was running toward them, jabbering excitedly about the bat exodus. BeeGee spotted him out of the corner of her eye and was about to explain that she'd suffered only from terminal surprise and a small loss of face when Dan kissed her.

There wasn't any warning before Dan's mouth covered hers, a much fiercer kiss than any other they'd shared. The bats were nothing compared to the shock BeeGee registered now. Her heartbeat never got the chance to slow back to normal. This was not the mere meeting of lips. Dan was all around her, his arms straining to hold her closer and closer to himself as if his body in a tight twining embrace was the only protection she needed.

She sure didn't feel tough, clinging to Dan. Her feet might have been on solid ground but her stomach took a sudden downward swoop and it was terribly hard to breathe. She was miles above the earth, gasping in a dangerously thin atmosphere, shivering in the heat. She didn't have to wonder anymore what it would be like if Dan kissed her without holding back. She knew.

His mouth was hot and hard and strangely sweet. There was a tensing of muscle in his back under the touch of BeeGee's fingers, a rippling that went right through her and a heated feeling that layers of clothes didn't stop. It made BeeGee want to melt right into him. When she clutched at him to hold the quick-silver sensation steady inside her, Dan made a little sound in his chest that frightened and excited her even more. His whole body trembled against hers.

He stopped kissing her and shifted himself slightly backward but he still held her, cupping her face and staring down. "Wow," he exhaled slowly. "Wow to you and whoa to me. Standing around doesn't get anything accomplished."

BeeGee would hardly have characterized what had just happened as "standing around" but she didn't argue aloud. Alex was right there, looking smug. Dan was already craning his neck and muttering about a plan of attack, getting the repairs done as quickly as possible. Maybe a kiss that wonderful and passionate only meant he'd got carried away. He was probably relieved she was okay and had not suffered cardiac arrest. Or maybe he was as surprised by an ex-tomboy's response as she was.

"Let's go," she said brightly, buckling herself back into the rig. "Up and at 'em."

Her enthusiasm won Alex's approval and a pat on the back but Dan frowned before he nodded agreement. It was hard for BeeGee to meet Dan's blue eyes straight on but she did. The bats were gone for a while but she now had to deal with a new threat. Dan was right next to her. If she was falling in love with him...

"Pretty brave, short stuff," Dan said in his usual way, and her thought receded. "What are you going for? A medal?"

"Early retirement," BeeGee answered as they made the ascent. "I don't want to hear about the bees. I want to finish this and get a hot shower, a big dinner. I don't want to see Dracula or Batman on the tube tonight."

He chuckled and they resumed work, laughing and making every bad bat pun they could think of. Alex sent up wire mesh to tack behind the replaced wooden louvers and solved the problem of keeping the bats out. BeeGee lamented the absent residents of the belfry; they'd lost their home, and even if they weren't good tenants they had been there, from the evidence, for a long time.

"This isn't supposed to be the First 'Battist' Church," Dan joked. "They'll have a new roost before dawn, believe me."

"Sure, but it's still a dirty trick," BeeGee said hotly, forgetting herself for a minute. "Everyone needs a place to live. I even hate to see kids stirring up ant holes and making the poor devils run around trying to save their little sand heaps...." She was getting carried away and as soon as she realized it, BeeGee cut short her tirade about homeless ants and bats.

Dan was shaking his head and looking askance at her. He remarked that for someone so tough she was also surprisingly tenderhearted, and BeeGee decided to leave it there. They were finished for the day and soon they'd be saying their goodbyes. The closer she allowed Dan to get to her, the more she would miss him when he left.

"Short work," gloated Alex as they both touched down and unhooked themselves. "I declare tomorrow a holiday!"

"We should have charged more," Dan said tersely.

"By the bat," suggested BeeGee with a laugh. She was now fully recovered from her experience, eager to tell her story to anyone who would listen. "We would have cleaned up on this job."

Alex liked the pun, but Dan had left his sense of humor up near the top of the steeple. He threw the gear hurriedly into the truck with a stony expression on his face. He had nothing to add to BeeGee's instant replay. When the loading was finished, he stood by the Bronco. His stiff posture and the hard, thin line of his mouth signaled his impatience.

"Oh, no. You two aren't riding with me smelling like that," announced Alex. "There's an old pump in back of this place. Go sluice yourselves off. We'll plan our celebration on the way back."

Dan slapped the metal fender with his hand and muttered something under his breath. "Come on," he said in a grudging tone to BeeGee. "I never knew Alex had such delicate sensibilities."

They picked their way through the overgrown vegetation, wading through the tangle of vines and bushes to get to the small cleared spot behind the church. At every step Dan complained about the insects that would probably devour them, the heat and humidity and the crying need for a decent gardener.

"I think a bat bit you," BeeGee said finally. "You're acting rabid." She ducked quickly to avoid being hit in the head by the mass of vines he released.

"Sorry!" There was no real apology in the word.

The pump was a genuine antique, rusted and complete with bucket and cup to prime it. The handle was nearly four feet long and promised to require the strength of Hercules to operate. BeeGee took one look at it and the junglelike setting all around them. She thought of snakes and shuddered.

"We could hitch a ride," she said feebly, "from someone with a head cold."

Dan jerked his thumb toward the pump, reached up with both hands and pulled his T-shirt off in one motion. He threw it on the ground and took a wide-legged stance in front of the spout, cupping his hands and holding them out.

"Subtle but effective," she murmured, throwing her entire weight onto the handle. It made a noise reminiscent of the bats and barely budged. She repeated the process until she coaxed a thin stream of water out. "I'd like to know what 'gator's nibbling at you. Something's chewing on you."

Dan was busy dousing himself all over, splashing his face and neck, chest and arms. He finished by sticking his head under the pump and briskly rinsing his hair. When he stood up he snapped his head back, surrounding himself with a million tiny diamonds of sparkling light, a brief shower of color.

"Your turn," he said brusquely, coming toward BeeGee to take her place.

Every time she went to the beach, she saw acres of male flesh displayed without effect. Seeing just one man's torso, naked to the waist, was different. He stirred thoughts and feelings deep within her. She wanted desperately to reach out for him, to touch the smooth golden expanse of his skin and fine curling hairs on his chest. Seeing Dan like this gave rise to a hundred new sensations, rustling like the leaves in the grove.

"Well, do you like what you see?" inquired Dan.

She went blank, unable to think of a clever comeback. Worse yet, BeeGee realized she had already given him the answer by her sheer inability to do anything but look. He was still approaching, slowly and deliberately, daring her to answer the question.

He wasn't smiling. "You've kept me at arm's length very nicely and very effectively for two weeks now. You're more afraid of me right this minute than you were of the bats. But why? You know I'm not going to hurt you, Ruth."

As if to prove his statement, Dan raised his hand and placed it lightly on her cheek. He let his thumb touch her mouth, rubbing it back and forth along her lips.

"Because I kissed you?" His eyes narrowed, probing the dark depths of hers. "I was worried. And it was wonderful, wasn't it?"

Yes, wonderful, but what did it mean? She wished she could ask him, but despite the humid, heavy air, her mouth was hot and dry. His fingers crept downward, stroking her throat and the small hollow at its base, feeling the pulse hammering there. He slipped the top button of her shirt through the buttonhole before she understood what was happening.

"Our business deal is concluded," BeeGee said in a throaty but firm voice. "Time for you to move on."

"You don't see me going anywhere," Dan said softly. "There's more between us than business. Or there could be, if you let it happen."

The second button opened as magically as the first. There was the cool touch of his fingertips hovering at the fabric's edge, ready to slide inside, but no movement. Dan did not look down at the open shirt, only into BeeGee's upturned face. She knew he must be reading all the confusion of desire and caution she felt so keenly.

"I'm not...not ready for more," she whispered, telling the truth and a lie in one breath. Everything about Dan—as a man, as a person—made her want more. Much more than he was offering. And she was not ready to hold him for today, losing him tomorrow.

"I am," Dan said fiercely. "I'm acting mean because I am. I'm getting crazy trying to figure you out. I never felt this way before and I'm not sure I like it."

His hands fell from the shirt to her narrow hips, clutching her without warning and bringing her to him in hard, intimate contact. BeeGee gasped, not just at the shock of impact with him but at the intense swirl of pleasure that danced through her.

"I want you as a woman," he growled, "and you expect to be treated like a kid sister. You got shaken up and I wanted to take care of you, make sure nothing bad ever happens to you." His voice lowered and swept through her like the breeze. "Ever!"

It was dizzying to be held this way, his taut body telling her of his need and his almost angry words telling her he cared, whether he wanted to or not. She wondered whether to cry or to kiss him...and did neither.

"Then let me go," BeeGee said, "and nothing will happen."

"Don't be so sure," Dan told her thickly, and he glanced down.

Her eyes followed his and she saw her own hand, palm flat, fingers spread wide, resting on his chest in the narrow gap separating them. She was touching him, not pushing him away. And it was very apparent that her own breasts, a few inches away, were equally bare under the open shirt.

Dan let her go instantly. BeeGee held the front of her blouse closed and didn't know where to look, what to say.

"And don't go shy or cold, either," Dan cautioned in a very gentle tone. "I'm not forcing anything to happen, am I?"

"No," BeeGee said with a hard swallow. No man with Dan's personality and real strength would have to force a woman physically. "I want to get out of here."

"Not before you do what we were sent for." Dan motioned her to the pump, taking in her look of wild consternation. "All right, don't panic. I'll look the other way like the perfect gentleman."

"Hardly perfect," BeeGee muttered, stepping around Dan. She stood and watched as the water began to trickle out. Dan made an elaborate show of twisting himself around, staring off into space and whistling loudly. "No, I haven't finished. I haven't started."

"Be quick," Dan ordered. "Even perfect gentlemen have only so much self-control." He moved the pump handle effortlessly but with a vengeance until he produced a gusher of only slightly rust-tinged water. He chuckled wickedly to himself and added, "Holler if you need help."

She could have cheerfully killed Alex for his suggestion. The water was so cold it stung her flushed face and throat like needles. BeeGee executed what must have ranked as a record for pulling off her shirt, washing off the thin layer of bat dust and drawing the shirt back on. She shivered violently, trying to button the shirt with shaking fingers.

"Better?" Dan left his post and retrieved his T-shirt, balling it up in his hand. "I hope my brother doesn't send us back to scrub behind the ears."

"I'll hold him down if you catch him," retorted BeeGee. She shook herself like a dog after a bath and followed Dan as he led the way out. When she was somewhere in the thicket, staring at Dan's broad naked back, a thought occurred to her. "Hey, how did you know when I was done? I never said..."

"Simple," Dan shouted back. "I peeked a couple of times."

BeeGee screamed at him, dredging up every unflattering description she could.

Dan was laughing when she crashed through to the church's front yard. "I *am* a perfect gentleman," he objected. "I never would have mentioned it but when asked, I was totally honest."

"My God, what took you so long?" grumbled Alex. "I didn't think you'd have to dig the well."

BeeGee hugged herself tightly and struggled for some composure. *Be adult about this,* she thought. She certainly wasn't the first woman Dan Greening had seen in a sate of undress and he hadn't been overcome with passion by the sight of her. In fact, he had laughed.

She stole a sidelong look at him as they all squeezed into the truck. Her sense of modesty and fair play was one thing; it wasn't the only thing. What would happen if she asked him if he liked what he saw?

"How about an outing to those islands you were talking about, BeeGee?" Alex was busy planning the next day. He volunteered Judy to pack a picnic for all of them. "We better take advantage of a day off and catch as much local color as possible before we leave."

"You'll love Sanibel and Captiva," promised BeeGee. She went on and on about the little islands stapled to the mainland by a steel bridge. They were heaven for shell collectors and wildlife enthusiasts. They were beautiful and unspoiled.

Alex was easily sold. He asked Dan if it sounded like a good idea to him.

"Okay with me," Dan said. "Of course, I take exception to BeeGee's chamber-of-commerce spiel about the prettiest sight on earth."

"Oh, naturally," she sneered, nettled by him. "You've been everywhere and seen everything, including the seven wonders of the world. Why not wait until tomorrow before you make up your mind?"

Dan shrugged, rubbing a bare arm along her. "I will, but I'm convinced I've already viewed the best Florida has to offer." He winked at BeeGee and grinned when she gave a demonstration of local color by blushing to the roots of her hair.

"I didn't think that much of Miami," Alex said, and gave the other two occupants a peculiar look when they both laughed at him.

Chapter Six

No detail ever escaped Emma Alden's critical eye. She looked BeeGee over like a jeweler appraising a large blue-white diamond.

"This must be some celebration to get you into a dress. You look positively...well, you're lovely in that color and it's very feminine. Now, just because I said that, don't run and change to your cutoffs."

"I won't," promised BeeGee. She took one last peek into the hall mirror, fluffing up the side of her hair and adjusting the straps on the pale blue cotton. She had bought the sun dress on an impulse when she worked at Markham's. There hadn't been more than two occasions since then to wear it. "You don't think it's too dressy, do you? White lace birds might be a bit much for island walking...."

Emma made a disgusted noise. "I knew it. I should have said you looked dowdy and dull."

"Okay! Okay!" BeeGee waved her hands around in frantic dismissal. "I hear their truck. I'm off."

She grabbed a scarf and her camera and kissed at the air right above Emma's cheek, hollering what time she expected to be back and what to say if this or that person called about a job.

There was the Bronco and Dan. No one else. BeeGee scrambled in, conscious that she was getting another inspection. His wide smile, the crinkling of the skin at the tilted corners of his eyes told her what his verdict was but Dan wasn't content with silent approval.

"I'm really flattered if you wore that to please me," he said. "Because it does. You are an awfully pretty woman, Ruth, and it doesn't hurt to let it show once in a while."

She accepted his compliment with a nod of her head and didn't bother to deny the reason she wore a dress. "Where're the others? I would have thought Kip would have been up at sunrise, hurrying everybody along."

"They're not coming," Dan said, keeping his eyes on the road. "I left them all sleeping. They can make it another day, I'm sure."

"That's weird," she commented. "Yesterday Judy was enthusiastic about an outing. And the food? Dan, I would have packed something for a picnic if you'd called and let me know."

"We'll manage. There are restaurants on the islands, aren't there?"

The truck was already on the narrow black ribbon of Route 867, heading southwest to the toll bridge. An uncomfortable suspicion arose in her but she managed to squelch it with thoughts of visiting one of her favorite spots. Dan was relaxed and cheery, handsome in a new short-sleeved shirt and khaki pants. He had also dressed for the day, trading his normal thick-soled ugly work boots for a pair of tan running shoes banded with blue arcs.

He was freshly shaved, freshly showered. BeeGee saw the small dark spots along his collar from his wet hair, a patch of red skin where he'd scraped himself shaving. The windows were rolled down but from time to time, she caught a scent separate from the sea: the lush banks of flowers. It was the clean, almost sharp smell she associated with Dan, neither strong nor sweet but wholly masculine.

"We're leaving in a couple of days," Dan said abruptly. "Heading up the coast to Sarasota. There's work there. Enough to do for two weeks, Alex thinks."

"Oh," was the most intelligent response she could think of. She found herself plucking at the delicate birds swooping across the skirt of her dress and folded her hands primly together in her lap.

"It isn't far and there may be enough to keep us busy for a month," added Dan. Not once did he take his eyes off the blacktop to glance over at her.

BeeGee cleared her throat, determined at least to sound conversational and casual if she couldn't muster enthusiasm. "That's good. A short trip shouldn't bother Judy, and Doc seems to think she'll be completely fit in another month."

"Well, how about it?"

Staring out the window without really seeing anything, BeeGee heard the question but it didn't connect. What did Dan want? Congratulations that they were leaving? She had known all along he wasn't going to stay. It was her own fault for sticking that knowledge way back into some dusty mental file and forgetting it.

"Yes, Sarasota's bigger and is probably full of chimneys and water towers," she said dully. "Kip will like the Ringling Circus Museum and Hall of Fame."

"Does that mean you'll go?" asked Dan. He stopped to pay the toll for the Sanibel-Captiva bridge. Chatting with the booth operator and getting a handful of brochures kept him busy for some time.

Only after they were speeding over the connecting road did he notice there had been no answer from BeeGee. He repeated the question.

"I heard you," she said irritably. "I'm thinking about it. Good grief, it's not as simple as a shopping trip. I assumed 'us' meant you and Alex. Dan, my business is here...."

She got what she expected. Dan raised one eyebrow and made a face as if she had just announced she was on a diplomatic mission from Venus. She could tell him she wasn't crazy, just scared, but then she'd have to tell him everything.

"You're not really swamped with work," Dan insisted. "A few more stints as steeplejack and you'd be ahead on your bills. We can use the help, you can use the money...damn, I thought you'd be happy, not grumpy."

"If that's a dwarf joke, it's not appreciated."

When in doubt, stall, BeeGee decided. He wasn't leaving immediately. At the least they would have today together, and she didn't want anything to spoil it. In a short time Dan had already given her some very pleasant memories, shared some of the best moments she'd ever known. Accepting his offer meant more time to be with him. Rejecting it meant more pain when he left.

Dan sighed loudly and dramatically. "Okay, think it over. I wouldn't want to rush you into something rash...like getting out of debt. Where do I park around here?"

It depended on what he planned to do, BeeGee said. There were only a few R.V.s and cars on the island today. Some visitors came for the wildlife haven, and as she pointed that way a flock of tropical birds rose, right on cue, and peppered the bright blue sky with vivid colors.

The beaches with incredibly fine sand and an inexhaustible store of shells attracted collectors from everywhere. Most tourists were interested only in filling their paper bags with souvenirs but there were also the serious treasure hunters in search of rare, valuable specimens. Today the beach was nearly deserted.

"You sound as though you memorized this brochure," said Dan, bringing the Bronco to a quick stop. He pulled out the keys and juggled them in his palm, making no move to get out. "It's not a bunch of birds I came to see."

She gathered up her camera, determined to be amiable. "I'd just as soon walk on the beach and look around. Hope you remembered your swimsuit. I'm sorry Alex and Judy and Kip couldn't join us. This place is my idea of paradise."

Her hand was on the door when Dan reached out and restrained her with a light touch. "I'm not sorry," he said very distinctly. "In fact, I asked them not to go today."

The confession and the slide of his fingers on her bare arm caught BeeGee off guard. She tipped her head to one side as if she hadn't quite heard him and looked at him out of the corner of her eye. "What? Why?"

"I thought it would be obvious. I wanted to be alone with you. There always seems to be somebody around when we're together. There's nothing wrong with wanting a little time for us—just you and me. Or is there?"

"No," BeeGee said with more conviction than she felt.

Hopping down from the truck, she slung the camera over her shoulder and slipped off her sandals. The sand was still pleasantly warm, not yet scorching. She hung the shoes by their thin straps over the crook of one finger and circled around to Dan, offering him her hand.

They walked a long stretch of the beach doing nothing more than enjoying the clear air, the brilliance of the water and the constant hum of the waves. Where the darker wet sands met the beach, there was a wealth of shells, washed in and left like a thin, wrinkled chain. BeeGee and Dan looked, but neither of them wanted to break the linkage of their arms to stop and pick up even one.

When they paused to watch an older man diligently sifting sand, Dan's arm circled her waist and hugged BeeGee to him. The expert collector glanced up from his patient examination of the sieve and gave them both an indulgent smile. Dan picked that moment to brush her temple with his mouth and when BeeGee looked toward him, startled by the contact, his lips found hers for a brief, light kiss.

"Have a nice life together," said the old man. "Here!" He grabbed up a large, round white object from the wire mesh and thrust it into Dan's hand. "It's for luck."

"Thanks," Dan grinned, and steered BeeGee farther down the beach. He held up the large, perfect sand dollar for her inspection. "We look like newlyweds, huh?"

She thought they might. The day was so exhilarating, the sun warm on her cheeks, the salty breeze full in her lungs. And Dan was with her. Every time she smiled at him, BeeGee was sure the way she felt about him must show. Even a total stranger recognized love when he saw it, even before the word had been spoken.

"Penny for your thoughts?" Dan tapped her nose with the sand dollar.

"I have very expensive thoughts," she retorted. "Your shell will buy you a race to that sign down there. Let's see what those fancy shoes can do, mister."

She had the sand dollar in her hand and was two quick steps ahead of him almost all the way. He was closing fast; BeeGee heard his breathing mixed with laughter. At the last second he grabbed for her, catching her shoulder and spinning her around. They both nearly toppled over in the collision.

"You cheated!" she puffed. "I nearly lost the camera...."

"I had to cheat," Dan said, holding tightly to her. "You always run away or edge away or back away."

She wasn't going anywhere. Even without his hard, muscular arm behind her to keep the length of her body next to his, she wouldn't have moved. There was no strength in her legs to run, no will to escape. It was much too wonderful and exciting to feel every lean inch of him, to see his eyes darken.

"Yes, I'm going to kiss you," whispered Dan. "I want to kiss and hold and touch you very much. Is that what you want, Ruth? You'd better tell me right now."

He gave her plenty of time to refuse. The descent of his face toward hers was slow—agonizingly slow. His very deliberateness and solemn expression made it plain that she would have to answer. She would have to admit what she wanted.

When his face was too close to see clearly, BeeGee closed her eyes. She could feel his warm, sweet breath on her skin and the steady, heavy pulse in his chest.

"Yes," she sighed. The regular rhythm of his heart and the faster flutter of her own combined with the rolling, endless song of the surf. By raising herself on her toes, by stretching to join her hands around his neck, she managed to close the tiny space between their lips herself.

At first the kisses were very gentle. His mouth brushed hers and left to travel slowly and rest lightly on her closed eyelids, her forehead and nose and chin. But always Dan returned to her mouth and each time he did, the bond was longer, deeper, more difficult to break.

When tenderness changed to hunger, BeeGee was ready. She found she wasn't even surprised or shy. Her own fingers were busy, stroking along the back of his neck and moving in his pale hair. Everything about him brought her pleasure: the fine texture of his skin, the rising heat of his body, the rich taste of him. All her senses were filled with Dan. There wasn't room to doubt this was right.

The weightless feeling was not imaginary. Dan had lifted her right off her feet, letting her toes wriggle inches above the silken sands. It took only one of his arms and the circle of her hands to keep them welded together. He had said he wanted to touch her and his other hand kept that promise, learning her contours by sliding up and down, across the thin cotton dress.

Her eyes opened and widened at the acute, electric messages his fingers transmitted to her. She was never before aware of how sensitive the small of her back, the taut curve of her buttock, the top of her thigh were. There wasn't a soul in sight but her involuntary gasp when his hand slipped around and up along her rib cage to cup her breast sounded loud enough to embarrass her and make her wonder who would come running.

"Too rough?" Dan whispered anxiously. He flexed his fingers, easing the pressure of his touch. "You're so delicate, Ruth. I'm almost afraid to—"

She brought her mouth to his, blocking the words. Experimentally, her tongue probed, returning the sweet, deep explorations Dan made. Her unexpected boldness did more than reassure him she was not objecting or in pain. Dan's knees buckled slightly and he reached up to disentangle her hands.

Lowering BeeGee and himself to the sand took no effort. She lay unresisting on an outstretched arm and Dan could kiss her and cradle her from the wind. She wanted her hands free to touch his face and arms and back. She wanted more than she would have dared to express, things she didn't even have a name for.

Dan buried his face in the soft, fragrant curve where her neck met her shoulder. He put his hand lightly over a hard little knot on her chest that showed through the material.

"Remind me this is a public beach. Tell me you are wearing something under that dress," he murmured in a way that was half joking, half serious.

"It is. I am," BeeGee breathed. She could have moved one of her wide straps aside and let him see the second-skin fit of her maillot but it didn't seem like a good idea.

Dan sat up and peered down at her. "You didn't, by any chance, want to act out the parts that nice old beachcomber assigned us, did you? The honeymooners?"

She shook sand out of her hair and brushed off the backs of her arms and elbows. Another shake of her head sufficed to answer his question and gave her heart a chance to resume a normal pattern. She wasn't in the mood to banter or be teased about what was very special to her, regardless of how ordinary this experience was for Dan. Knowing the day of his departure made today more poignant, more difficult.

Dan stretched out on his side, propping his head up on one hand. With the other, he scooped up some of the moon-pale sand and let it sift back through his long, tanned fingers. When it was all gone, he opened his hand and showed her a very small, perfect whelk left in his palm.

"What a beautiful place," he said. "You can find a treasure without really trying."

BeeGee glanced at its banded pink-and-purple markings and went back to watching the waves. "It's pretty but it's common, Dan."

"I wasn't just talking about the shell," he informed her softly. "I meant you, too. You're special. You're a treasure."

"You don't know—" she began to say, but a dry, tight stricture cut off the words. She was reduced to shaking her head from side to side and working hard at not crying.

"I do know. I know you are brave in situations that would make most people feel faint and terribly scared. You like to act tough as nails and you don't know when you are being so sexy that a man nearly has to tie himself down...."

"Me?" She had to remind herself to close her mouth. Once she saw his face, she could not force her eyes away.

"It wasn't any Amazon in a negligee who raised my blood pressure a few minutes ago," he said with a crooked smile. "It was someone who doesn't know how she looks in a white T-shirt and faded jeans, especially when she bends or reaches for a brush. Sexy, as in the ability to put certain thoughts in my head by the way you laugh or move or look at me. Inexperienced, too. You don't know as much as you think you do."

"There are a few gaps in my education," admitted BeeGee.

"A few big gaps! And in your life?" guessed Dan. "It's not usual to be adopted at seventeen or called by a nickname that's almost an insult. And you get shy or defensive at the oddest times." He sat up again and dusted away the sand clinging to him. "I want to know you, Ruth, but you have to trust me here just like when we're dangling sixty feet off the ground.''

He was the only person, apart from the Aldens, who called her Ruth and she liked the sound of her name when he said it. She took a deep breath and risking it, told him all about being Baby Girl Chambers.

"I wasn't wanted, to begin with. That's why my mother never bothered to give me a real name. She kinda dragged me around after her for years until the authorities made a point of taking me away. I bounced through a lot of places after that. Foster homes, agency placements, juvenile halls. They were pretty bad and I was worse. I kept running away.''

Dan took her hand and the gesture made it difficult for BeeGee to tell him more in a flat, controlled voice. She didn't want him to feel sorry for her. She had been wild and unmanageable, she said, and it wasn't necessary to gloss over it or make herself seem pitiful.

"You're hardly pitiful,'' retorted Dan. ''Now I know how you got so tough. Not just climbing trees, was it?''

"Fences, fire escapes, sneaking into warehouses and running from anyone wearing a uniform,'' BeeGee listed, ticking the offenses off on her fingers. ''I must have covered more ground in those years than the Greenings ever did in their trailers. I got thrown off a Greyhound for not having a ticket, headed for Miami when I was sixteen. Right here, in Fort Myers. I was standing in the dust, wondering whether to walk, steal or hitchhike, when the Aldens wandered by and offered me a meal.''

The rest of the story was the easy part to tell. With their own children grown, the Aldens took on BeeGee, asking no questions but giving no quarter. Within a year she was in school, filling in the gaps of her erratic education and thinking of the Aldens as her family.

"I nearly drove them crazy but they hung in there. And I really wanted to stay. They were the first real parents and this was the first real home I had. That's why the adoption was important. It was symbolic. I was almost legally on my own but I needed to belong."

"Thanks for telling me," Dan said. "Things make more sense."

"What? No questions?" BeeGee smiled but she didn't feel especially lighthearted. The usual reaction would be a hundred questions. Didn't Dan want to know how wild she had been? A typical male response was to turn aggressor and to treat her as if she had nothing to lose.

Dan stood up and pulled her to her feet. He appeared to be thinking about questions for a few minutes but then shook his head solemnly. "No questions! I'm not who I was five years ago, either. I don't expect to be the same man five years from now. If you want to know me, you have to judge who I am today. Everything I said about you still goes. It's what I've seen these past two weeks."

They resumed their walk. She felt special and treasured with Dan. It was more than relief at finding someone to be open with and more than happiness at his acceptance of who she was. She nearly told him she loved him, but he had been right about her shyness at the oddest times. The words buzzed in her head but never quite made it to her lips.

Suddenly, Dan stopped walking, bent down and made horrible growling noises while he pretended to chew on her shoulder. "I'm starving!" he complained. "All this healthy exercise and sea air give me an appetite... and about a ton of sand in my shoes."

She promised him there was a restaurant close by if he could hold himself in check for five minutes. "I hope you brought money so we don't have to dig for pirate doubloons or do dishes." She put her hand in her dress pocket and pulled out the sand dollar. "This is not going to pay the tab."

"My treat! Over a genuine business lunch, tax deductible, we are going to hammer out a deal for Sarasota and I am going to eat an entire whale, French fried." He laughed and started to take such long strides toward Mario's Seafood that BeeGee had to run to keep up with him.

"I didn't say I'd go," she hollered at his broad back.

"You will," Dan shouted with infuriating confidence. "I'm known far and wide for my powers of persuasion."

A warning light went on somewhere in her brain. A little of her buoyancy ebbed away. From what she'd told him about herself, she thought he'd understood her situation perfectly. Fort Myers and the Aldens were all she had and all she'd wanted until very recently.

Her footsteps slowed. Dan was far ahead, waving her anxiously on and trying to make her laugh by pretending to be weak with hunger. Sarasota was only the next stop for him in a long series of stops. He took his home and his family with him like a turtle carrying his shell. Her life and her world were here.

Chapter Seven

His protective feeling was back, stronger than ever. Dan could sense a tinge of possessiveness, too, that bothered him. He waited for BeeGee at the entrance of the restaurant and took her arm, not just because he was doing the polite thing or because it made him feel good to touch her. The unvarnished truth, if he looked into the more shadowed parts of himself the same way he was peering around Mario's dim interior, was complex, disturbing.

"I want to sit by the windows," she said in hushed tones to him. "Can we?"

It was the shy little nuance Dan picked up on now and understood. A fancy restaurant awed her; she was not used to luxury and not sure of herself in unfamiliar settings. Linen tablecloths and napkins, fresh flowers on a table, a waiter who spoke with deference—the things Diane had taken for granted, as her due, were still slightly foreign to the woman who stood next to him now.

"Let me ply you with liquor," said Dan, ordering a Mimosa and a beer from the hovering waiter. "I used to be an expert at the standard martini-and-hard-sell lunch."

BeeGee was peeking around, admiring the fabulous ocean view through the wide windows shaded by awnings striped in green, white and orange. Her fingers lightly, unconsciously ran over the silver scallop shells topping the place settings.

"In season, you have to wait in a line that goes out the door," she said. It was an attempt to appear easy and knowledgeable, and for the first time, Dan knew it. The enigmatic mixture of old and young, shy and bold, childlike and wise: he could finally put the pieces of a puzzle called BeeGee together and see a full picture.

"You come here often, mam'selle?" He also knew his lousy French accent slayed her and he wanted her to laugh, not to be awed or uncomfortable.

"I was here with Doc and Em for my birthday. The big one, number twenty-one."

Dan asked her when her birthday was. Two weeks earlier he hadn't known she existed. Two weeks later he was aware of what amused her, what certain sounds she made meant, what a tilt of her head conveyed, but he didn't even know her birthday.

The drinks came to their table and he offered a toast. "I wish for you what you wish for yourself." He meant it. He'd never wished anyone more success or happiness than Ruth Chambers because he'd met very few people who deserved it as much as she did.

Her candid story of herself, so painful and revealing, brought Dan face-to-face with all the enormous differences in their lives. Starting with nothing, feeling like no one with nowhere to go? Unbidden, the image of Diane Mather flashed into his mind. Having the best of everything didn't produce any notable strength of character, just a manicured, elegant, complacent kind of beauty.

BeeGee sipped the orange blossom cautiously and rubbed her nose when the champagne bubbles tickled. "I'd like this orange juice straight," she admitted.

Dan smiled and waved the waiter back. "You're not a drinker or a smoker. But I heard a few choice words slip out when you were being dive-bombed at that church."

"My only bat habit," she grinned, but it faded fast. "No, I take that back. I'm a bit of a gambler, too. Every once in a while I bite off more than I can chew but Sarasota sticks in my throat. Bad odds."

He wasn't sure what she meant. It was a great job, close by and lucrative. Sarasota was practically a hop, skip and a jump from here and they could call all the shots: starting time, hours per day, extra help. Dan detected a glaze creeping over her eyes, a deliberate inattentiveness to his description. She wasn't asking questions or showing any interest.

He was irked. "You aren't listening to me! You have nothing big or pressing in the works right now but you won't even listen."

"I can't take off for two weeks or a month and expect to have a business. They want you when they want you or they call someone else."

There was more to it than that. Dan let her know he wasn't buying any glib or lame excuses and waited. She had shown such overwhelming trust in him on the beach. Why was she stopping short of the truth about this?

"I'm not worried about breaking my neck, if that's what you think," BeeGee added uncomfortably. "But there are risks . . . no, I meant reasons. There are reasons."

"Name two." He snapped a bread stick in two and menaced her with one piece.

"I lost my wanderlust when I came here and I haven't gone anywhere since," BeeGee said with a shrug. "You may not have noticed but Doc and Emma are old. Doc will be seventy-two next month. They rely on me. They need me here. . . ."

Dan's disgusted slap on the tablecloth made the silverware jump. "I wasn't suggesting you enlist in the foreign legion. Sarasota is right up north on this coast. Did I say the Sahara, by mistake? You can drive back on weekends."

The waiter returned, showing more teeth than the shark in *Jaws*. "Are we ready to order?"

"Only if I can order this woman to think straight," said Dan. "Ruth, you really struggled to get as far as you have but you're limiting yourself. This far and no farther. Can't you see that?"

"Give him the crab special," BeeGee said to the waiter. "It suits him."

"Give her the shrimp plate," Dan responded without missing a beat. "She thinks small."

The poor bemused man scribbled on his pad and scurried off before they could correct each other. He swooped back briefly with bread rolls, and gave them both a nervous glance.

"You can evidently do anything you put your hand to," Dan was hissing, trying to keep his voice down. "You just won't think big, expand your horizons. You're free to do whatever you like. As the saying goes, you're a big girl."

"You move around to feel free. I moved around searching for a place to belong. That's the difference." BeeGee stabbed at her salad, wondering why it was as easy to fight with Dan as it was to kiss him. Fighting wasn't nearly as enjoyable but it was almost as exciting. "Before I say yes or no, I want to look at every angle."

"Including the man-woman angle," Dan said knowingly, and smiled when her fork clinked on her teeth. "Yes, sex still worries you. The prospect of us living and working together..."

The arrival of the food was timed perfectly. The curious waiter wasn't going to leave without hearing about her prospects, if he could. He fussed and swept away invisible crumbs.

"I'm not living with you," gasped BeeGee. "Your powers of persuasion aren't that good!"

"Living close together," he amended swiftly. "You'd stay with Alex and Judy." It was all planned, neatly worked out, without BeeGee's knowledge or consent. She could have the couch or share Kip's room. To hear Dan explain it, the possibility of her refusing to go hadn't crossed anyone's mind.

"The shrimp are small but they're delicious. Try one," offered BeeGee as he launched into the financial reasons she should go. Dan must have been great at talking people into real-estate investments; in a manner of speaking, she was considering buying land under a foot of water from him. She could break her heart, if not her neck.

"You're small but delicious, too," Dan said softly. "I was heading back to that angle. The attraction between us is powerful and mutual. I want to make love to you but the decision has to be mutual. You can stop worrying about a seduction scene in Sarasota unless you want one."

His bluntness was refreshing and reassuring. Nothing was going to happen that she didn't want. Dan rested his case when BeeGee insisted she would think about Sarasota and give him a definite answer very soon.

"Not another word about this for the rest of the day," BeeGee said fiercely as they got up to leave. "Or I'll kick down your sand castle."

"Is that the only option for this afternoon?" Dan asked, slipping an arm around her waist. "I was hoping for a little wading, a little swimming, a little..."

"Yes?" BeeGee was nodding agreement to each phrase. "Picture taking?" Holding out her camera, she looked up at him. "Buying stuffed alligators with felt hats? Postcards?"

"A little more kissing," Dan ended with a demonstration, outside of Mario's. "This is not to sway your decision. It's pure selfishness on my part."

The second kiss was entirely mutual.

Discussion, questions and plans melted in the broiling summer sun. When the real heat of the day set in, it made the air sway and shimmer, playing tricks on the eyes. BeeGee ran ahead, frolicking with a stray dog. To Dan she became a mirage, blurred and indistinct. She and the mutt changed to dark elusive shapes against the blinding, white sands, and just when Dan started to be taken in by the illusion, she reappeared.

"No," he said before she had a chance to ask. "I'm not taking that woebegone beast back with us. Look, he's already found another playmate."

There was something terrifically fragile and vulnerable in her eyes. "He needs a home...."

She was no longer masking or shielding things from him, Dan thought. He'd won her trust but the whole concept of winning and losing was no longer clear to him.

Two weeks before, it had been a simple matter. He'd geared himself up to make a pass at her and be encouraged or rejected. The night she'd sat for Kip,

BeeGee had been part of a game like Crazy Eights and he'd known the precise moment he had broken a cardinal rule and begun to care for her.

"Take your clothes off," begged BeeGee. She was struggling out of her dress and weighting her things down with the camera case. "I'm roasting. I have to take a dip. Hey, don't you know how to swim? Don't just stand there waiting for heatstroke!"

"Tell me to get undressed again. I really like the way that sounded." He stripped off his shirt and started to unzip his pants, waggling his eyebrows lasciviously at her. She got flustered and tried hard not to show it. "Now who's standing there and staring?"

She fled, a lithe, scantily clad nymph, into the white-and-silver foam of the waves. He could catch her but then he would have to deal with the confusion she raised. This was an infatuation, nothing more. He kept changing his plans and breaking his own rules to be with her a minute longer, a day more. Maybe making love to her would end it, wash her out of his thoughts and system the way a plunge in the waves cooled the fever in his veins. Infatuation, like lust, burned itself out.

She was floating on her back right over the next swell with the ease of a tiny dark-eyed seal. "I was beginning to think the crab plate gave you cramps and I ought to start a search for you." She gave him her imitation of Emma Alden. "Never swim an hour after lunch or you'll sink like a stone."

He got the humor and understood how much maternal concern touched BeeGee. It was ludicrous to try to warn her about the dangers of jaywalking after she had experienced firsthand the terrors of hitchhiking, sleeping in deserted buildings, outrunning persistent lawmen.

"It's the sharks," Dan called. "I was slow because I wrestled a huge white one. Punched him in the nose seconds before you were a particle between his teeth."

"Oh, pooh!" She kicked up a shower to keep Dan away. "There isn't a shark in a thousand—" Something grabbed her heel and pinched its way along the back of her leg up to her knee.

She let herself be dragged down and seconds later emerged in his embrace. There was nothing awful about this shark devouring her, their wet skins slipping on each other and their laughter being carried over the waves. Her own ability to wrestle sharks was considerable as she showed him, diving under and rendering him helpless with a combination of tussling and tickling.

"Beaten by a slippery octopus," gasped Dan, dragging her out of the water. "I give up. You win. Do with me what you will."

To his delight, she flopped down next to him and kissed him with unbridled enthusiasm. He loved the way her kisses revealed how new this all was to her, how he had to take her hand and put it on his chest to show her that men liked to be touched and shared certain responses with women. She encountered the small, hard male nipple and there was wonder in her face.

"If we don't build a dopey sand castle soon," he said after some longer, deeper kisses, "we'll either get arrested or get sunburned in some interesting places. I am about to peel off that suit and these trunks, Ruth."

Wisely, she scooted away and he willed the ache of desire in his body to ebb. It wouldn't entirely leave him, and Dan sensed that if he left Fort Myers without her, she would haunt him. His infatuation hadn't run its course.

"Smile!" she ordered, fumbling to focus him in the camera lens. "You look slightly pained, Mr. Greening."

"I am," he groaned. "I am. How is it possible for you to drive me half-crazy and not know it?"

She drew her dark brows closer together and frowned, intent on her picture. "I don't know. I thought you were crazy from the day we met and I don't notice any difference today."

"Well, thank you!" He put his head back and laughed, feeling far more calm and composed when she wasn't testing his restraint or his sanity.

For one brief but genuinely crazy minute, he had asked himself if he was in love with BeeGee Chambers, smashing the final dictum he had set for himself years ago. No, being with Diane Mather brought him a wonderful calm and peace. He had known Diane two years and Ruth two weeks. Love was against the rules and love at first sight was nonsense.

"It was a great day."

Emma Alden laughed. "I think I've heard that somewhere."

"About six times in the last hour," remarked Doc. "Have we missed any detail?"

BeeGee didn't bother to add certain footnotes. The Aldens could not be as entralled by a description of Dan's physique in swim trunks as she had been. They wouldn't gain much by hearing how often he had reached for BeeGee or how many excuses they had found for touching.

"Dan did ask me about taking another job," BeeGee said, setting her giddiness aside. She outlined the offer as calmly and objectively as she could, hoping, their reaction would tip the balance one way or the other.

"My, my, you've impressed them," was Emma's sole remark. "Are you going soon?"

Doc was less help. "Sounds good." He polished his eyeglasses with deep concentration and then rested them on his head, not on his nose. "Glad things fell into place for them."

"I wanted a bit more of an opinion," admitted BeeGee. "We don't have to vote on it, but normally I get an earful on which hardware store to go to."

"All right, Ruth," sighed Doc. He picked up the large sand dollar she'd left on the coffee table and flipped it to her. "What's inside?"

"Me or this shell?" she asked.

"Both," he answered.

By shaking the sand dollar, BeeGee satisfied herself. It wasn't necessary to crack open her souvenir of Sanibel. She had broken other sand dollars in sections to find the small white bird-shaped pieces inside. There were usually five tiny birds but she didn't want to ruin the old man's gift just to check.

"The doves are there," she told Doc. "I can't tell you for sure how many or how big but they're there. As for me, I don't know. I'm confused about what I want to do but I'm not convinced picking myself apart will yield any answers. I asked you and Em for advice to save myself the trouble of digging around, breaking myself apart and coming up empty. Or worse, with a bunch of disagreeable new problems."

"That's the dilemma for most of this whole blinking world, in fact," said Doc. "Whatever's inside us stays trapped and untapped because we aren't willing to open ourselves and risk further change."

"I'm talking about a *job*," cried BeeGee, frustrated. "I don't want to sacrifice my business here for a few weeks' work out of town. If people call and I'm not here . . ."

"They'll wait or they'll get McKeon's Fix-it," countered Doc. "You wouldn't agonize this way if it was *only* a job. You're a bird afraid to leave the nest, Ruth, and try your wings."

"Are you and Emma pushing me out?" She felt a moment of childish panic and let it pass. "Do you want me to leave?"

"Of course not, honey." Doc put his arm around her shoulders and hugged her. "When birds want to fly, you can't stop them unless you cage them. When they're not ready, a push generally means they'll resist or fall." He took his hand and closed it over hers and the sand dollar. "You've only been here a few years. We had the other Alden nestlings for ages, it seemed. Em and I pegged you for a late bloomer."

"I'll be ready to try overnight camp by my late thirties," teased BeeGee. She rested her head on Doc's shoulder, admiring his incredible patience and wisdom once more. "I'll marry at fifty."

Doc chuckled wickedly. "You'll be ready sooner than that. Em and I are speculating on what will happen when you fall in love. And we know you are rather taken with Dan Greening. Nothing like love, BeeGee, to inspire changes."

"Dinner!" chimed Emma from the kitchen. She prudently left the serious discussions to Doc, knowing her own tendency toward browbeating.

BeeGee refused to consider eating. She was still a shrimp stuffed with shrimp, she claimed, and she had a decision to deliver by morning. She took her sand dollar and herself out to the porch for heavy-duty thinking.

In the hours she sat there, BeeGee wasn't grappling with Dan's powers of persuasion. He wanted her to go, Doc and Emma wanted her to go, she wanted to go but not wholeheartedly. The decision was unanimous but uncomfortable. Intellectually and financially, there was not a single good reason to refuse. She was going to pay an emotional price but a businesswoman, even a budding one, knew costs had to be figured into every human transaction.

Her fingers gripped the sand dollar so hard it cracked in two and fell from her hand onto the wide porch boards. BeeGee bent down, feeling for it and gathering up the shattered remains. The memento of a flawless day was ruined. She could find only two of the shell's inner treasures; a tiny pair of white birds that fit comfortably on her thumbnail. The others were lost or broken.

Doc had said it all. It was time to try her wings. She wasn't leaving the Aldens forever. She wasn't being offered love forever from Dan. Starting as a hard-headed survivor, BeeGee saw tonight how the smooth, protected years here made it more and more difficult to take risks, to be hurt. Well, she was going to get hurt sooner or later by Dan Greening. He never mentioned love except linked with another woman's memory.

Sarasota could be a real opportunity to grow up. Her ledgers showed the uneven progress of the past two years. Financially, she would come back rich enough to start even. She would be with Dan for however long it took to finish the contract, testing her independence and the depth of her feelings for him. And she could move back, but only a little, to the way she once was—fearless, nothing to lose, a defiant kid in mud-caked sneakers—without losing any of her sense of worth and purpose.

A noise made BeeGee start violently. She saw Emma's face assume an expression of outrage and at the same time noticed the sky was light.

"Yes," she said loudly to cover Emma's grumbling inquiry. "I sat up all night and will catch my death of cold. It's a well-known fact. I will go and shower now and put on clean underwear in case I get into an accident."

Emma followed her into the house and up most of the stairs, asking for an explanation for her inexplicable behavior.

"I'll pack this afternoon for Sarasota," BeeGee promised, leaving a trail of clothes from bedroom to bathroom. "You're going to have to take messages for me during the week. On the weekend I'll get back here and take care of any callers."

"I heard exactly the same line when LaVonne left for college," chuckled Emma. The rush of water and the slam of the shower door did not stop her reminiscence. "She came home three times the first semester and with her future husband in tow the second."

"What? Did you say something?"

"Not a blessed thing," shouted Emma. "We'll talk when you're dressed."

Fashion spoke louder than words to Mrs. Alden. When BeeGee came downstairs, she was wearing a white-and-mauve print skirt and a mauve T-shirt, cut high on the arms and low in the back.

"You look so pretty," commented Doc over the top of his *Courier*. He retreated when his wife wagged an eyebrow at him.

"If you're planning on traveling in that outfit in your truck..." Emma protested.

"I'm leaving tomorrow," corrected BeeGee. "I'm going to a business meeting now."

She was well aware of their fishy looks and inaudible comments as she left. They were partially right if they thought Dan was the impetus for this transformation. She was content to look like a grubby urchin when she worked but her all-night brainstorming made her see the necessity to change her thinking and her style.

The facade of a dirty face hadn't kept Dan from seeing her as an attractive woman. She might as well stop using work clothes and a peeling, freckled nose to mislead men into accepting her as "one of the guys." The only acceptance that counted was the acceptance of herself as a woman.

The torn upholstery of the truck seat was filthy. BeeGee walked the mile and a half to the trailer park, pleased with herself for all sorts of reasons. She laughed when Judy opened to her knock and did an elaborate, dramatic double-take.

"Mother of pearl! You came to say thanks but no, thanks. *Vogue* offered you a modeling career and you don't want to play monkey with the Greenings anymore."

"Midgets aren't high fashion," pouted BeeGee. "I'd have to be as tall as you and weigh as much as Kip. I decided I'd rather do what I do best than suck in my cheeks and look bored. I'm going!"

"Did you hear that?" cried Judy delightedly. Alex and Kip were inches away and couldn't have missed it. "Dan will be happy and unbearably smug. He said you'd go and after all the arm twisting he did to get Alex to agree and to set up the details with the factory... whoops, I blabbed."

"You sure did," thundered Dan's voice from behind BeeGee. He pushed her ahead of him into the room. If he was angry at his sister-in-law for revealing how much trouble it had taken him to cook up a scheme to keep BeeGee with them a while longer, the anger was tucked away for another time. He picked BeeGee up and swung her around, making the skirt flare and Kip giggle at adult foolishness. "Saddled up and ready to ride, huh?"

"Not quite," said BeeGee, getting dizzy from the circles he swung her in. "I need to talk about the details, not dance the waltz."

While the serious matters of money and living arrangements, the kinds of tools and techniques they would use were being settled, she secretly savored the flattery of Dan's eyes with the knowledge that he had engineered a job to include her. It was heady stuff to be looked at as if she was truly beautiful while she was being consulted and listened to as a competent craftsman.

"I'll haul the muriatic acid in my pickup," agreed BeeGee.

"Dan has to drive with you," Judy said, out of the blue. "Alex can drive this silver beast with a rented rig and I can handle the small trailer with the Bronco."

"You shouldn't have to drive," objected BeeGee. "Not fifty, not a hundred, not even one mile."

She was voted down. Judy displayed a note from Doc Alden to a doctor in Sarasota that she claimed was a clean bill of health. Her blood pressure was fine. Her only restrictions were to continue to take things easy and to limit her ice-cream cravings to "three fla-vors a day."

At her first chance to confront Judy alone, BeeGee peeked out at Alex and Dan flipping a Frisbee to Kip and read the riot act to her. "You're playing Cupid and you'd better stop," she threatened. "It's not what you think, Judy."

"I don't think. I know," Judy insisted. "I'll help it along all I can because you are what Dan wants and needs ... and you're a pretty neat prospect as a sister-in-law, even if I couldn't borrow any clothes."

"Was Diane in Detroit closer to your size?" asked BeeGee with a flippancy that wasn't real. "Oh, yes, I've heard about her and the highest tower. I can be a chimney-sweeping sidekick or 'fun and games' but it's highly unlikely I'm more than a passing fancy. I'm coming back here in a few weeks."

Judy was plainly disappointed that Dan still thought, let alone talked, about his ex-fiancée. She didn't have a single nice thing to say about Diane, even with an English muffin loaded with jam to console herself.

"It was a dirty trick for her to change her mind at the last minute," groused Judy. "She knew for months what we were planning to do. She got cold feet, not just about marriage but about what her wealthy friends and family would think if she went through with it. Diane was helpless, couldn't screw a light bulb into a socket. Marry a man who works with his hands? She was one of those very smart, decora-tive women who go first-class. Maybe she thought

Dan wanted her to be able to do something blue-collar, besides dazzle him.''

"Ouch, you're mean," BeeGee said. She slipped into the strange position of defending someone she didn't know or want to know. "Isn't it possible she couldn't leave and give up everything for his love?''

"Anything's possible," Judy replied cynically. "She loved him to distraction when he was grossing six figures, played tennis and was planning a European tour with her. Forget that Dan hated what he did and didn't ask her to be more than what she is this very minute, wife and mother.''

BeeGee could forget it; Dan was the one who couldn't. Matchmaking was strictly out, she told Judy in her hardest tone. Despite Judy's tendency to blab, it felt good to confide in another woman and talk about her own limits. BeeGee would never be as open as Judy, most likely, but she'd discovered this new freedom to say what weighed her down, and it was a refreshing start.

"I'm determined to grow where I was finally planted.'' BeeGee finished telling the pertinent facts about herself and smiled, seeing a friendly understanding had been reached. "I read and watched 'Roots' with a special bias. I didn't have a clue as to who I was until five years ago. Talk about a late bloomer!''

"I was a teacher. I see a quick learner," said Judy.

The day went by as fast as a summer squall, yet placidly. BeeGee hung around to help Judy organize the move, lifting heavy boxes and emptying the refrigerator. Dan and Alex were too busy to do more than chat for a few minutes. During the afternoon they emptied the refrigerator in their own way.

When Dan took BeeGee home, it was not quite dark but her eyelids kept sinking and her arms and legs felt leaden.

"I didn't sleep much last night," she confessed. "I wasn't as sure I was tagging along as you seemed to be."

His kisses were like snowflakes tonight. They fell on her face with the softest touch imaginable and melted away before she knew they were there.

"I didn't sleep much, either, and it was all because of you," whispered Dan. "I hope I don't howl every night in Sarasota, thinking about you alone on the couch next door."

"I won't be alone. Kip has lent me my choice of his stuffed animals, with the exception of one-eyed Tenmoo, whoever that may be."

"There is a wonderful sound tires make on the highway," Dan said to BeeGee the next morning as they headed off. "I listen carefully, but it never lulls me to sleep. It's beautiful and I've missed it."

BeeGee put the pickup into overdrive and the humming of tires, the throbbing of engine changed abruptly. She knew what Dan meant. A few times since she'd taken the wheel she'd heard herself begin to sing, fitting names from the road signs to music.

Charlotte Harbor was not pretty or singsong like Matlacha, Solano or Gasparilla. BeeGee caught sight of the water and tried to include it in a lyric. It was a bowl of cobalt blue shimmering off to her left and flowing right under a span of North Forty-One.

"Murdock, Murdock 'round the bend, been there once and going again," BeeGee chanted.

"When were you in Murdock?" Dan gave her a teasing swat with his baseball cap. "Judy told me you've never been to half the places right around here."

"I was *through* Murdock four years ago. I was through about a million garden spots," snickered BeeGee.

"I know something BeeGee can't do," Dan said as they whipped past Murdock. "I finally got one."

She was stumped after rhyming "things" with Warm Mineral Springs. "Rings? Warm Mineral Springs in your bathtub leaves rings. Name one thing I can't do, copilot."

"You can't carry a tune in a wheelbarrow," groaned Dan. "It is a shame and a pity. You get so much volume and so few right notes." He stuck his head out the window and cried for help in a pained tone.

"Professional jealousy, petty rivalry," BeeGee said, undeterred. "I'll let you off and you can wait for the rest of this troupe to pick you up. Or look! There's a blonde in a new Corvette. Pull up your pant leg and catch her eye with your hairy ankle."

Her eyes drifted to the blonde but Dan's did not. He was seemingly more interested in teasing her and enjoying the ride than admiring the panoramic scenery or the stunning driver of the other vehicle. BeeGee stared, though, as the sportier car flashed by. Did a certain Diane have long pale ribbons of hair streaming out behind her when she drove?

"Stop it," she heard herself say, and had to squelch the thought while making up a quick poem for Dan and keeping her eyes on the road. She was happy. Why spoil it with envy?

"I wasn't criticizing," he laughed. "I was gloating. It'll make me insecure if you really can do everything. Male ego bruises easy."

"Bandages are in the glove compartment."

Chapter Eight

Sarasota was a vacation. BeeGee didn't admit it aloud but it wasn't a very well-kept secret. The first few days were allotted for "getting set," as Dan termed it. The translation of that phrase meant that he, Alex and Kip went to softball games and fishing while she and Judy had the entire day to themselves.

"This is *me*," said Judy, holding up a maternity top with ice-cream cones printed all over it. She spread the voluminous gathers beneath the yoke and speculated on how many months and gallons of ice cream it would take before she measured up to it.

"You're over your nerves," remarked BeeGee, "if you're buying this new wardrobe. I wish I could say the same for myself."

"What? That you're pregnant?" giggled Judy. "I'm sure it can be arranged."

"No, thanks! Not quite yet," BeeGee assured her. "I'm one of the old hard-liners. You know, marriage, then making love and making babies. I mean, I drove out to the factory site with Dan yesterday afternoon before we did the shopping. I saw those big chimneys and my jitters came back. I thought they'd vanished. Especially after surviving the bat attack."

Judy put down a stuffed unicorn, which continued to tinkle out a music-box version of "The Impossible Dream." "You can't still be jumpy about working the height," she said with authority. "If you are jittery, look for another cause." She gave BeeGee a sly look. "He's a foot taller than you, twice your weight."

BeeGee changed the subject. "You must be going, pardon the expression, batty about now. When do you think you'll be able to work up there again? And for how long?"

Judy strolled down McKinney Boulevard without answering. She had to stop at every interesting shop window to admire the windup swings and cribs and folding strollers. Finally, she sighed and turned to BeeGee.

"Don't tell Alex," she warned, "but I haven't missed the steeplejacking as much as I thought I would. The jobs have gone smoothly without me, thank goodness...and you. And I love spending all this time with Kip. I may just have to tell Alex to start figuring our future jobs on the basis of a Dynamic Duo, not the Terrific Trio."

"Would that be all right with them?" BeeGee was incredulous.

"Sure," said Judy with a little wave of her hand. "From time to time, Alex gets a bug in his ear about doing something different himself. One year he was going to be a chinchilla rancher. Last summer he conceived some plan to make his fortune with an earthworm farm. Well, I'll have plenty to do with a new baby and teaching Kip every day."

Her comment reminded Judy to find the educational-resources store she had looked up in the phone book. Her experience as a teacher in Michigan allowed her legitimately to teach Kip at home but he was progressing faster than she expected. There was a constant need to get him new workbooks and materials.

"And he really has a head start on geography," teased Judy. "How many little kids can find all the places they've been to on a map?"

"I couldn't," admitted BeeGee ruefully. In fact, she couldn't even remember some of them. It was probably for the best. She may have moved around almost as much as the Greenings but she hadn't done it with the security of a loving, stable family, as Judy's and Alex's children would.

"Well, time for lunch," announced Judy. "After that, we'll go home and plan tomorrow's agenda. I think we should all go to the circus museum, don't you? Even the two big clowns will like that."

"We had lunch," BeeGee said. "You won't have to worry about telling Alex you won't climb anymore if you put on eighty pounds."

They laughed and devised an imaginary crane system to hoist a tubby Judy onto the top of buildings. BeeGee knew she was going to miss Judy sorely after this job was over. The Aldens' own children were grown and gone when she had arrived on the scene. Judy was becoming the sister she'd never had, the best friend she had missed making during her years of rootless living.

There was an excursion to the Ringling Hall of Fame and a few side trips to see what Sarasota had to offer. But there was also the factory and three massive brick chimneys. BeeGee wondered if some of her growing reluctance to start the work wasn't due in part to the knowledge that this was it. This trip was not a vacation but her final stint as a steeplejack and the last she would see of this extraordinary group of people.

Her reluctance was rapidly diminishing in another area, however. The physical relationship with Dan was deepening, becoming as necessary to her as the need to breathe. It did not matter if the day's work left her bone weary because there was Dan, her source of renewed energy every night. The minute they were alone and in each other's arms, she forgot fatigue. More and more, she considered forgetting caution.

Untutored and inexperienced as she was, BeeGee sensed how extraordinary and special a lover Dan would be. His greatest pleasure seemed to be in finding a way to make her sigh with delight, take her slowly to the very borders of ecstasy to see what waited for her when she was ready.

There was always his patience, the whispered question, "Do you like this?" And his mouth or the slide of his fingers across silken skin created such havoc within her that BeeGee could hardly speak.

She said she would watch a movie with him but the images flickering across the television screen were going largely unnoticed. Nestled together on the couch in his trailer, there was nothing more compelling than him.

"Tomorrow's Friday. Do you want to quit a few hours early and drive back for the weekend before the heavy traffic?"

Leave? Leave the intoxication of these kisses, the drugging comfort of his arms? She had left Fort Myers with a reluctance she thought would last and protect her from forgetting how temporary everything else was.

"I'll call Em again in the morning," BeeGee said. "She kept telling me there wasn't anything going on, anything urgent. I got the impression I wouldn't be missed if I stayed."

"You'll be missed if you go."

It was sheer heaven to hear those words. It was heaven to let him push her back gently into the cushions and fit their bodies together. The weight of his body was not a crushing burden, although she teased him about it. He held her down but the sensation he aroused was one of soaring.

"What are you looking at?" she asked. His face hovered over hers far too long, not lowering to fill the yearning that hollowed her inside. She touched his mouth once in appeal.

"You know how much I want you," Dan said softly. "I see it reflected in your eyes. Aren't you wondering how long you can play with fire and not get burned?"

His fingers stroked down along the arched column of her throat and rubbed the ridge of her collarbone. He bent his head to kiss the spot and leave his damp, heated brand behind.

"You won't hurt me." BeeGee used his own words with all the assurance of a sure thing. She believed him. Dan never pressured her to go too far, too fast.

His hands grew restless and searched for the hem of her blouse to tug it free from her shorts. He raised his chest from her, allowing the material to move upward. The movement rocked their hips into total contact, a pressure so shocking but deliciously pleasant that BeeGee gasped a bit. Dan stopped and then moved again very slowly and deliberately.

He watched her face, eyes widening, mouth slightly parted. "Hot enough for you?" he whispered hoarsely. The phrase must have been used ten times a day since they'd arrived but it meant something worlds different now.

There was a wildness, a darkness in the depths of his eyes and she was being drawn into it. Without her willing it, BeeGee felt her body lift to meet his. There was fire in her and every caress of his insistent hands on her skin made it blaze hotter.

The final fuel was his mouth, igniting a passion she never suspected could burn so brightly. His kisses were rougher than any she remembered. The rhythmic probing of his tongue matched the powerful, primitive appeal of his movements, the thrust and retreat of his hips.

"Dan," she moaned, a cry to be loved and consumed in flame. "Oh, Dan."

The sounds were strangled under the seal of his mouth but he heard. He understood. For a minute, longer than any she had ever known, Dan clung to her so tightly she could feel his whole body trembling as with great effort, their hearts pounding with mutual madness.

"I can't," he said in an anguished voice. "I thought I could but I can't."

The throbbing sensation of his body on hers told her he could indeed complete her, make her his in the ultimate, intimate sharing between a man and a woman. But something else had happened. He did not even look quite the same when he sat up hastily and raked his fingers through his hair over and over.

"I was going to show you how dangerous this all is," Dan muttered. It sounded to her as if he was clenching his teeth. "Show you? Ha! There's a funny line about a joke backfiring but it escapes me...." His voice trailed off and he turned toward her.

She thought she was in shock. There didn't seem to be any feeling in her hands and feet. With the excitement drained, there was numbness and sadness. She saw his attempt to smile and tried to return it. Neither of them did a creditable job.

"I guess I do see," BeeGee said finally. "When my restraint is down, yours takes over. Lucky me! Most men don't think it's a big deal, being the first man...."

He hadn't asked her that question but she had just given him the answer. He'd known. He'd known all along, somewhere in his guts more than in his head.

"It's a big deal," Dan said quietly. "It's too important for me to be casual with you and for you to think it's just because we got a little crazy." He got to his feet and held out his hand to her, helping her up. "I can only say I'm sorry. I don't want to sleep with you if I end up hating myself tomorrow morning. You may not think you'll hate me now, but you will."

"Will I?" She managed a real smile this time. She tried to picture herself hating this thoughtful, tender man but it was impossible.

Dan jerked her chin up a bit and grinned. "You know the expression, 'hated with a passion'? You don't need a first lover, Ruth. You need...hell, you *deserve* a first and only and forever lover. And if I'm aching right now, I deserve it and worse. It's just fun and games to me, you know that."

She wished with all her heart she had the nerve to ask him why his eyes looked unhappy, desolate. "I'll stick around this weekend. But we better call it a night now."

He walked her to the door with a companionable arm draped around her. "Alex and I are going bone fishing tomorrow. You're welcome to join in.'' The kiss he planted on her nose was comradely, brotherly, anything but the kiss of a lover.

"It's a dirty job but someone has to do it!'' Dan grinned and swiped a fast forefinger down the front of BeeGee's nose.

The chimneys had an elaborate new internal system for filtering out soot and impurities. The top of the stacks, however, were still ringed with heavy deposits of fly ash and carbon black from previous years. Every trip skyward to work on the bricks meant coming down speckled and streaked.

"There're birds' nests up there,'' BeeGee informed him. "Boy, I'm glad it's not hatching time. I wouldn't have the heart to move them out.''

Her face itched. Every time she scratched it, Dan and Alex got hysterical. After she saw what she looked like in the truck's mirror, she laughed, too. Besides the broad stripe down her nose, she was a mass of squiggly black lines and dots.

"If it weren't for the glamour, I'd never do this silly work,'' chortled BeeGee.

"You're okay! You're a sport,'' said Alex.

"You're more than that,'' Dan offered, wiping some of the soot away with his sleeve. "You're pretty wonderful, BeeGee.''

At that moment, with his eyes and his touch as soft and loving as she'd ever known, BeeGee wished time would simply stop. She could have stood there forever, smiling up at him, almost sure that the next words would be the very ones she wanted to hear.

Every morning this week, she'd received a ritual kiss from Dan before they started. Not once, other than that, had he touched her. He wanted to. She could read certain looks across the dinner table, she noticed the way he watched her when he thought she was busy with Kip or Judy. But for all this time, they had been "buddies" and nothing else.

"Hey, guys, we could be finished with Old Smoky if you don't take the rest of the day off," complained Alex.

It was true but finishing the job didn't sound like much of an accomplishment to BeeGee. She ducked her head and got back into her harness without a word to either of them. Completing her section of brick-work kept her hands busy but it couldn't completely occupy her mind. She had made a mistake following them here.

Glimpsing the highest tower and falling in love with Dan was a disaster. She would not even be close enough to him to sustain her dreams after today. He was right; the risk wasn't worth the feeling of being suspended between heaven and earth with no place to go.

Dan flicked a tiny piece of wet mortar at her. "That's it!" he crowed triumphantly. "Alex, you done?"

There was an affirmative from Alex and an ear-splitting yodel. "We're the greatest!" A frightened bird made a wide detour overhead when the three trespassers laughed and cheered. If there was a slightly hollow sound to BeeGee's voice, no one noticed.

"How about a night on the town?" Dan asked her as they tied up the loose ends. "I feel like dancing."

Her dark curls caught the fire of the setting sun as she shook her head vehemently. "Not me. I have other plans."

"What plans?" Dan grabbed her before she could walk off. "Judy and Alex won't be offended if we skip the family banquet. We'll bring back a bottle of champagne for them."

"I don't feel like celebrating," BeeGee ground out. "I . . . I'm tired. Yes, that's it. I'm tired."

He brought his face very close to hers. "You, tired? Have you got a headache, too?" His eyes were alight with mischief, and the ends of his mouth curved in a mocking smile.

"If you want to kiss, don't mind me. I can turn around and look disinterested," chuckled Alex.

"I don't want to kiss," BeeGee said. Her mouth formed a straight line.

"Speak for yourself. You always do." Dan smudged her cheeks with his soot-coated hands as he held her face and tilted it firmly upward. "Here's to a job well-done." He planted a kiss, light and casual, on her tightly compressed lips. "And to a new champion steeplejack." The next kiss was a little more insistent, a little more difficult to resist.

She responded, ignoring the very reasons she shouldn't. She kissed him back, letting her lips slacken and welcoming the taste of Dan mingled with a bit of ash. Having Alex as a witness did not stop her from embracing Dan with passion seasoned by sadness. This was her last chance to hold him and kiss him.

"And to a partnership that works," breathed Dan before he claimed another kiss. His hands were sliding up and down her back, molding BeeGee to him.

"Don't forget Groundhog Day, either," said Alex loudly. "The signing of the Magna Carta is worth a squeeze, too." He got noisily into the truck, leaving them alone.

"I could think of a lot of reasons to keep doing this," whispered Dan. He nuzzled the side of Bee-Gee's throat damply. "This might not be the right place, however."

The place suited her because they had run out of time. She would be throwing her few things together that night and leaving in the morning. Her fingers wanted to stay locked around his neck or knead the round, knotted strength of his shoulders.

"How about one for the road?" she asked boldly, and ran her tongue tentatively around the rim of his ear.

The effect her request had was rather startling. Dan's body stirred unmistakably and his mouth was on hers with a hard, grinding demand that stole all the air from her lungs, all thoughts from her mind.

"Oh, God, Ruth," he groaned. "I should never start something I can't finish. I want you so much."

The reason for Dan's careful behavior with her this last week was no longer a mystery. He was attempting now to make up for days of controlled longing.

BeeGee was shaken, unsure either of them could handle the fires they set so easily in each other. She felt the heat in her blood burn away her final reservation and allow her to say what she had longed to before. It was too late. It didn't matter.

She twisted away from the consuming hunger of his mouth. "I love you," BeeGee said. "It doesn't change anything but I want you to know that I love you."

Dan took a single deep breath and let it out slowly in a long exhalation, saying only her name. He touched her cheek once with his fingertips and let his hand drop to his side. He didn't chorus the sentiment; she didn't expect him to reply.

She was glad the words were out. The old habit of running and hiding from people, from herself, was almost completely broken with her simple declaration. Dan spoke only of wanting, not loving, but at least they were both dealing with the truth.

She had fibbed about being tired before. Suddenly, she was exhausted. On the ride back to the trailer camp, BeeGee let her head sink to Dan's shoulder and closed her eyes to shut out the glare of the sun on the horizon. Her appetite for small talk and dinner had vanished.

"School's just about out," Judy said to them. She and Kip were studying at the kitchen table, sorting through a pile of cardboard letters to spell his daily quota of words. "We got a late start today. Kipper and I had to hit the circus museum once more for another poster."

"Sounds great." Alex threw open the refrigerator with a proprietary air. "I'll do the dinner while you two finish. We had an early and fine ending to the job. My incredible omelet or shrimp creole?"

BeeGee was already down the hall and pulling out her suitcase. She would get through dinner for form's sake and make the goodbyes as short and sweet as possible. By the time she had washed up and changed, the aroma of a spicy sauce was drifting under the door.

Alex directed her to the table with a wave of his spoon and went back to studying some papers stuck in his other hand. When Dan came in, he was called over immediately to see the letters. There was a minimum of conferring and both men joined BeeGee, Judy and Kip for dinner.

"Well, does it meet with your approval?" asked Judy, pointed to the papers Alex had shoved aside.

"Taste the shrimp first and see how you like it," advised Alex.

It was delicious. Everyone agreed it was fabulous, inspired and most edible. Dan kept smiling at BeeGee across the centerpiece of carnations and baby's breath, Alex's bouquet to Judy. BeeGee had the distinct feeling she was missing something vital. Why was he so happy?

"I thought it was a great deal," mumbled Judy, helping herself to more rice. "They've made all the arrangements for a two- or three-month stay, trailer space provided. No expenses to speak of. Why, they even offered me the company's nursery school for Kip's social life.''

The pieces fell into place for BeeGee. ''Your next job,'' she said to no one in particular. ''That was fast!''

''I've been thinking...'' began Alex in a peculiar tone of voice. He sounded like a politician about to make a speech. ''It's going to be different when there are two children, Judy.''

Judy looked at BeeGee and sneered. ''I knew this was coming. I hear this stuff twice a year. Alex wants to buy a dude ranch or a fish hatchery and it's going to be *my* idea!''

Dan laughed at his brother's offended look. ''She's right, Alex. You'll be the problem, not the kids.''

''Me? I want to consider a regular school for Kip, a nice garden for my wife with a jungle gym for the kids.''

Judy began to defend her ability as a teacher and her love of travel. She hated gardening, she claimed. Alex countered but BeeGee got the idea that this really was a familiar mock argument, an exercise for each of them.

Dan confirmed it by leaning over and whispering, rather loudly, footnotes to the heated discussion. ''If he keeps this up, Judy's going to mention Chinese pizza.''

Alex cleared his throat and took out his letters to tap the table for emphasis. ''Here's a very good deal and it would be a challenge.''

"We'll take it," interrupted Judy and Dan in chorus. BeeGee smoothed Kip's golden head and felt her eyes sting.

"I was thinking of a small family restaurant," said Alex dreamily. "My specialities would be—"

"Chinese pizza," intoned Judy. "It gives you indigestion an hour later."

"I'll reconsider," muttered Alex, unfolding the letters. "It's a lot of money."

"Show her. Show her." Judy hit Alex on the top of his head in passing. "Don't sit there like a miser hunched over, counting his gold."

Alex grimaced and handed the letter over to BeeGee. She skimmed down details of how many chimneys so high of such and such a type and configuration. It was an enormous undertaking, one of those lengthy jobs Dan had talked about. And it was in Dayton, Ohio. After she saw the city and state on the letterhead, she didn't care to read the figures but she was obviously expected to make some congratulatory comment.

"Oh, great!" came out of her mouth with the same cadence and feeling as if she was saying, "Oh, death!" Something was dying, after all. It was the end of her brief steeplejacking career and the end of her hopes. She couldn't look at Dan.

"I still think I should open a restaurant," Alex was saying. "After a meal like tonight's, why should I deprive the world of my talent?"

"Excuse me," BeeGee said thickly, pushing herself away from the table. "I want to check the oil in my truck before it gets dark. I'm going to leave very early...."

"Honey, I think it's raining," Judy insisted in the midst of her renewed fight with Alex. "Alex, be reasonable. You would eat all the profits. True, we wouldn't starve to death but ..."

BeeGee fled. Another minute and she would be in tears in front of all of them. It was not quite raining yet outside but the storm would be there before long. The sound of thunder assaulted her eardrums and the trees were shuddering, bending with every gust of cooler wind.

Dayton, Ohio. Why not the moon? It was nearly as remote and strange. BeeGee wrapped her arms around her midriff and hugged herself as tightly as she could. She paced briskly back and forth in front of the trailer until she heard the door opening. She would sit in the pickup and wait or cry. She couldn't bear to face them.

"Where are you going?" Dan shouted. "Ruth?"

She lengthened her step, pretending she didn't hear. It was easy with the boom of thunder and the sighing of the first wave of rain. The drops fell gently, pattering into the dust, dampening her. She almost broke into a run, determined not to make a scene.

"Wait a minute." His hand caught her, spun her around. She tried to pull away and found it useless. "What's the rush? Have you got a heavy date?"

Sarcasm was fine with BeeGee. His impatience and anger, too. It would make it much easier to say goodbye.

"Yes, I do," she said in a tightly controlled voice. "The Fort Myers Debs Cotillion is tomorrow...."

Dan actually shook her, to her amazement. Not hard but he jiggled her arms as if she was a puppet. "You don't drink, so you're not drunk. What the hell is wrong with you?"

You, she should have said. Instead she snapped, "You're hurting me."

The rain was harder now. It fell faster in long slashes that were rapidly soaking them both. Dan let go of her and ran his hand over his face, flicking off the rain.

"Sorry," he said. "If it's all the same to you, I think we can go in and discuss this where it's dry."

BeeGee took a step backward. "It's not the same to me. I have nothing to discuss and I'm not going anywhere with you." Saying the words unleashed the tears. They were hot and the rain was cold on her face.

Some of his confusion lifted. The bewilderment that clouded his blue eyes disappeared and they took on a hard, determined gleam. "You didn't give me a chance to ask. There was a reason for you to read our contract. You're part of this team and you could be part of—"

"No!" shrieked BeeGee over the howl of the wind. She thrust her arm out in the general direction of Fort Myers. "I have a home. H-O-M-E. I have a family there. Have you forgotten? I can't commute from Ohio to Florida on weekends."

"Damn it! Shut up," ordered Dan. Even as he started to argue with her, the full strength of the storm hit. Sheeted rain slapped them and the violent gusts of air whipped most of his words away.

They faced each other, drenched and dripping, each unable to hear what the other was saying. The dusty ground was rapidly soaking up the downpour, turning into a bog. Dan's mouth was moving while water ran down his face in steady rivulets and he made wild, uncoordinated gestures with his hands. In the midst of her own fury, BeeGee was seized with an uncontrollable urge to laugh.

They must look demented, she suddenly realized. Leaning forward to brace herself—and to jab him angrily in the chest—her foot nearly slipped out from under her on the mud. They were fighting like the proverbial wet hens, just as mad, just as mute.

Dan must have come to the same conclusion. He tugged at her sleeve, neatly plastered to her, and started to smile. There was a moment of wordless communication and agreement. They both made a run, sliding in the slick spots, toward the trailers.

Naturally, she headed for Pegasus and a change to dry clothes. Dan had other ideas. He dragged her in the direction of his smaller trailer, leaving two shallow ruts from her feet to mark their progress.

"Oh, no," he hollered at her as he fumbled with the door. "I don't need Alex and Judy to referee this one. This is between you and me." He pushed and pulled until she went inside.

BeeGee locked her knees and set her jaw, standing in a growing circle of water on the small entry patch of tiles. "Fine," she said, keeping her teeth clenched to prevent chattering. "I can tell you in three words. I'm going home."

"After the hospital," he added. "We're going to die of pneumonia and make this whole conversation moot. Let me give you a towel or something."

"I'm wash and wear. Just throw me in the dryer for a few minutes," suggested BeeGee, beginning to shiver. But she let him haul her along, wailing about the muddy footprints they were leaving on the carpet.

"Here!" Dan blinded her by throwing a bath towel over her head and led her into the next room.

She dutifully rubbed her hair and peeked out. His bedroom was larger than she thought it would be. Dan was riffling through his clothes closet and emerged with a brown terry-cloth robe. He threw it on the huge bed and laughed aloud.

"You look like a drowned rat," he said sweetly. "I'll go change in the bathroom while you put that on. Shall I make a pot of coffee?"

"Only if I can sit in it," murmured BeeGee, too cold to object. She waited until he took one step out of the room and then stripped off all her clammy clothes. Everything from her skin out was soaked.

His robe was warm and soft and smelled like Dan. Putting it on was like surrounding herself with him. BeeGee swam in the folds of it, rolling up the sleeves and wrapping it around her. The belt alone would circle her twice and the hem brushed midway between her calves and ankles.

She patted at her hair and wandered around his room, unabashedly snooping. There were a few photographs on the low teak dresser but they were of Kip and an older couple she assumed were the elder Greenings. There were no sleek blondes in evidence who left men stranded on love's pinnacle.

She peeked behind the curtains and saw the rain still hitting the window. A flash of lightning made her jump and drop the drapery back in place.

"And in this corner, at ninety-five pounds, in the brown bathrobe, Kid Chambers," said Dan from behind her.

"You could knock," BeeGee objected, spinning around. "I know we've been great buddies but I'm not really a kid."

"You sure aren't," he agreed softly. "Maybe that's why I didn't knock first. I've peeked before, haven't I?"

She didn't answer, although the memories of the little grove and the pump behind the church flooded her mind. Didn't he understand it was all over? She was going back where she belonged and he was going ahead with his life.

He came closer, his bare feet making no sound, his unbuttoned shirt revealing his bare chest. "Maybe there's a better way than mud wrestling, of making you understand why you're expected to go with us," he said in a very low but clear voice. "It's more complicated than just working well together. Let me show you."

Chapter Nine

The rumble of those words was echoed by more thunder. Dan's bedroom was lit eerily with another jagged lightning bolt. His face and torso were illuminated by the purplish white blaze, reminiscent of a flashbulb's lingering glow. BeeGee knew she wouldn't be able to forget this moment, a mental snapshot of this man she loved and was leaving.

"I said..." Dan started to repeat his invitation while he advanced toward her.

"I know what you said," BeeGee roared, with a storm raging in her. "There's nothing you can show me but the way out. Whatever you have in mind will make things more complicated than they already are. There's you and me and this bed. I'm afraid we will both want to simplify what's happened in your way, not mine."

His arms opened to receive her and she pushed them away. Her mind wanted to close out the raw appeal of his face.

"Where are my clothes? My shoes?" She tried to inject her words with the coldness of the rain outside.

"In the washer. You can't go out like that." Dan stepped backward, keeping her in sight and not letting her get past him. His arm came up to bar the doorway. "I don't want you going anywhere but Dayton. Is that uncomplicated, plain enough?"

"Yes," she hissed, determined not to lose the sharp edge of anger. Anger would keep her moving; love would make her crumple. "It's simple and cruel and impossible. Ohio is what you want."

"Then tell me what you want." His arm fell limply by his side. "Tell me what's wrong with Ohio."

"As far as I know, nothing. But Sarasota is as far as I go. Physically and emotionally." She had to take gulps of air between phrases. God, why did he have to make goodbye this hard? Her voice quivered and broke. "I told you I loved you. I told you ... too much."

She could bolt out of the room and run. Instead, she covered her face with her hands, as lost in the enormity of her feelings as she was in the folds of his robe.

"And I haven't told you very much," Dan said quietly. "All the trusting and sharing of confidences has been pretty much one-sided."

Dan went to sit on the edge of the bed. There was no sound except the chugging of the washer's motor and the slashing beat of rain on the trailer. When BeeGee took her hands from her face, wiping away the evidence of tears, and twisted her head to see him, he seemed oblivious to her. He kept raking his fingers through his hair; the light tousled strands were the only bright spot in the gloom around them, drawing her eye, making her long to smooth them down.

"I'm going just as soon as I can," announced BeeGee. She observed the restless progress of his fingers that didn't cease. "You and I can't work out the tangles between us."

His nervous gesture stopped. "We might. We've been good for each other. These past few weeks have made me aware of how lonely I've been sometimes. I realized how close my thirtieth birthday is, how much I envy Alex having Judy and Kip and a new baby on the way. I should say, *you* made me aware of those feelings."

She became conscious of holding her breath, afraid to look at him, afraid to hope.

"If this is love," Dan continued, "it will grow and mature but I want to give it more time. Let's be sure. I bought us two weeks, setting up Sarasota. I even stayed away from you physically this past week—as much as possible—because I realized that I could never turn my back on you if I made love to you."

Her chest hurt and she was beginning to get light-headed. "I understand. While you make up your mind about us, I'm supposed to tag along and help. I know how I feel but I'm not going with you. I can't be in two places at once. I have a prior commitment to Doc and Emma, to myself, and everything solid and stable and permanent is just down the road. But not in your direction."

"What if we got married? The ultimate partnership... you'd go as my wife."

He was actually frowning when BeeGee turned and looked at him. She was horrified and infuriated. Hadn't he understood a single word she'd said? Her soul had been laid bare and Dan chose to think she was wangling a marriage proposal, asking for a better contract.

"What is this?" she screamed. "'Let's Make a Deal'? You'll marry me, unsure of your feelings, and hope or pray I grow to fit into Diane's shoes. Ruth Ellen Chambers, runner-up to Miss Highest Tower!"

His head snapped up. Dan got to his feet. BeeGee fled into the hallway to get her clothes and get out. She threw one soggy sneaker at him with every intention of bouncing it off his thick skull. Dan fielded it and kept coming, his scowl giving him a truly fearsome aspect.

She was beyond reason and fear. He only looked like the Viking conqueror, she thought as she tugged the sodden mass of clothes free. It was impossible to unknot his jeans from her shirt and hold the robe closed at the same time but she discovered she was past caring about modesty.

"I won't marry you or any man who thinks the open road calls," BeeGee snapped. "I sure as shooting wouldn't marry anyone to be second-best or a clause in a business contract."

"There's no one lower than a man who hits a woman," Dan said grimly. "Keep this nonsense up and I'll settle for shaking you silly."

She threw the damp mess down and put her hands on her hips. The defiant pose coupled with the contemptuous lift of her chin opened the front of the terry-cloth robe wider. She was too far gone to be aware of the provocative revelation of one startlingly white breast with its sharp contrast to her tan and her taut rose nipple.

"Don't settle for less than you want," she taunted him. "I'm telling you I won't settle. Not anymore. I'm already settled down. I'm not a rich socialite but I'm not a dumb hick kid, either."

"I'll say," muttered Dan. He looked at the tiled ceiling as if imploring heaven.

"Bigger men than you have tried to slap sense into my head and failed," growled BeeGee. "They couldn't catch me."

"Thank goodness," he whispered helplessly. "Ruth, if you're finished, I would appreciate it if..."

"I'm not doing you any favors. I'm clearing out."

"... If you'd close that robe and let me discuss this face-to-face," he said in a huge rush. "I'd like to think of myself as a rational, mature male. However, my blood is boiling, my hormones are acting up and I am getting a severe crick in my neck."

Silence greeted his announcement. Finally, a much chastened, normal voice said, "Okay."

Dan took a few steps forward, rubbing the back of his head. "I'm going to put these things in the dryer. You can't drive safely when you're all riled up. The rain is slowing down, I'll set the dryer on high and we'll both find a neutral corner while you're waiting."

Regally, she stepped over the laundry and without a backward glance made her way into his living room. While Dan fiddled with dials and slammed lids shut, she tucked her feet under her and buried her hands in the sleeves. The situation was defused, although she was still not sure how it had happened. With anger gone and nothing more to say, she was left with sadness and resignation.

She'd be sensible and mature, too. She'd stay until her clothes dried or her maturity ran out, whichever came first.

Dan must have been thinking along the same lines. They spent a very subdued hour drinking coffee and staring mutely over the rims of their cups at each other. Conversation was so deathly polite it hurt.

Changing in his bathroom, she glanced at a different BeeGee in the mirror above the sink. The experiment to test her wings had failed; she looked bedraggled and worn.

"I'll say goodbye to Alex and Judy and Kip now," BeeGee said when she emerged. "You don't have to walk me over."

Dan nodded and took her hand, neither handshake nor caress. They stood as immobile as statues, searching for words or a way to make the last moment, at least, right.

"Take care of yourself," Dan ordered roughly. He started to say more but decided against it, closing his jaw with visible effort.

I'll miss you. I'll never forget you. I love you. She thought her farewells, unable to utter them. A final kiss, no matter how fleeting or friendly, was out of the question. She would humiliate herself with more hysterics.

Somewhere on the highway, hours later, BeeGee realized she had absolutely no memory of her leave-taking with the other Greenings. What was said or done was lost. The clearest picture she could conjure up was of herself telling Dan she could not be in two places at one time.

Wrong. At every fluorescent mile marker, she was reminded she was wrong. When she was back in Fort Myers where she belonged, sneaking silently through the dark house and avoiding the tread that creaked, she knew she was wrong. A part of BeeGee was with Dan, laughing and holding him, and could not be separated by the lonely black ribbon of highway or the hours she had driven. Torn in two, she blamed no one but herself.

She was here but her heart was there.

"You've got to see Mrs. Bleeker. It's urgent." Emma took the untouched breakfast away from BeeGee without comment.

"It's her floor," she replied, scanning part of Doc's paper intently. "I'm doing it today."

There had been no inquisition, as BeeGee had dreaded. For the past week there had been a scrupulous avoidance of the whole subject of her return. She was grateful for that, because her black cloud of depression had not yet lifted. Going through the motions seemed to satisfy everyone and BeeGee had decided that when she was ready to talk, she would.

"Bill. Bill. Junk. Letter. Bill. Postcard," recited Doc, sorting through the mail. He flipped the postcard to BeeGee.

She squinted at the tightly packed message, deciphering Judy's handwriting with difficulty. When she put the card down, there were two sets of eyes fixed on her. Em's mouth was pursed and her cheeks puffed as if she was about to burst. Doc rustled the newspaper but he didn't turn a page.

"They arrived intact," BeeGee said evenly. She didn't feel it was necessary to say who was the subject of her explanation. "There are sufficient chimneys and ice-cream parlors to keep an army busy. Kip has a girlfriend with dark hair at the community center and Judy swears she is the spitting image of me. She's probably as tall as me, too."

"Very newsy," said Em. She folded her arms and tapped a finger in expectation of more.

"Judy and the baby and all, are they well?" Doc was a bit more subtle. He hit "all" hard for emphasis and left it at that.

"She didn't mention Dan," BeeGee replied, pushing back her chair.

Emma Alden stiffened and thrust her head forward. "You don't say! Well, why should she? You don't mention him, either."

"He's history." BeeGee felt that if she talked very fast it would be over sooner. If she sounded cold, perhaps the ice would cool her emotions. "I wasn't very good in history, you might recall. I could be there in Dayton. They... he asked me to go. He asked me to marry him, too, in a roundabout way. But, as you can see, I'm here. The end."

"You were never much for public speaking, either," grumbled Doc. "There's better coverage of Mother's silly garden luncheon in this local rag. Dayton? Marriage?"

"I don't want to talk about Dan," said BeeGee. "I don't even want to think about Dan but I can't seem to shut my brain off."

"It appears to me that you have," Emma commented with a rare bit of sarcasm. "I liked Daniel Greening very much but that's neither here nor there. You better think more, not less, about him and start acting normal again. He's not history, Ruth; he's current events."

She was not going to be forced into a discussion she wasn't ready to cope with. BeeGee stalked out with the postcard clutched in her fingers. Her era of frequent squabbling with the Aldens had ended long ago. They rarely fought about anything or seriously disagreed with her. It galled her to think a mere mention of Dan made them suddenly question how well she was handling her problems.

She really thought she had fooled Doc and Em. She might as well give up trying to fool herself. While hammering on the Bleeker floor, it made sense to thrash out her own miseries and put her life back in order. Judy's standard line of "Wish you were here" had stirred up a huge new wave of longing.

Crawling around seemed to mirror her spirits and BeeGee was about as low as she could get. She scrambled on her hands and knees across the floor she was marking for a new tile covering. Pounding down stubborn nail heads until they disappeared into the shiny fiberboard surface was almost therapeutic, especially when she accompanied each stroke with a succinct comment.

"Dumb. Dumb. Dumb!"

There was a good ring of truth to that one and it applied equally well to both of them. She really must have been dumb to imagine Dan would give up his life style to please her. In all honesty, his work, his travels, his whole outlook suited him. Part of his attraction for her had been his total satisfaction with what he had carved out for himself, his disregard for what other people expected of him.

"Free! Free...as a...bird!" She gave the nail a particularly vicious swipe and bent it over into a useless curve.

Well, they were now both free to follow their own flight plans. Eagles soar and sparrows don't migrate, she thought philosophically. Dan was probably a thousand miles away or a hundred feet up in the air, swinging through the sunshine. The light would catch in his hair, a golden flash as bright as the gleam from the steeple's cross. She missed the nail by a fraction and hit herself on the hand.

"Shuckadarn," BeeGee swore. She sat bolt upright and examined the damage she'd inflicted on herself. Even back in her own safe nest, her mind was still off wandering with Dan. And thinking about Dan was just as dangerous, just as hopeless and not as much fun now as it had been when the traveling was real.

"Having trouble? Need help?"

His voice! BeeGee skittered around on her backside and stared at the screen door. She put her bleeding knuckle in her mouth in the time-honored tradition of children soothing their hurts. A cut healed. Even her heart would mend, but not if Dan was going to appear from time to time to make it ache again.

He opened the screen door and took a small step into the Bleekers' kitchen. It wasn't like Dan to walk so tentatively, BeeGee noted to herself. He usually took long loping strides as if he was racing to catch something. Or someone.

"What are you doing here?" she demanded. There were two sorts of pain to deal with and the stinging in her finger was the least worrisome. "Dayton, Ohio is that way. Did you make a wrong turn? Forget something?" She pointed in the general direction and saw his smile begin to form.

"Both," Dan said with a little laugh. He came a little closer and looked down at her, extending his hand. His eyes weren't laughing, however. "It might take a while to explain. You have got a few minutes to spare, haven't you?"

"Only until my war wound stops throbbing. Mrs. Bleeker told me her husband has conniption fits if his dinner isn't on the table precisely ten minutes after he ambles in from work. I've got three hours and twenty-seven minutes to peel and stick the most gosh-awful orange-and-blue tiles you've ever seen."

BeeGee didn't take his hand. She couldn't. It was hard enough to see him again and chatter nervously and pretend it was really okay to be with him. A touch would be asking—no, begging—for trouble.

"Okay, but this isn't exactly the setting I had in mind," Dan said amiably, joining her on the floor. He had no difficulty folding up his long legs, draping his bare muscular arms comfortably over his knees. "You have a real talent for changing my plans. I sort of pictured that nice seafood restaurant out on Sanibel, candles and lobsters, wine and soft music."

"They don't have music," BeeGee reminded him tersely. She looked away from him to the ugly wallpaper she'd just been paid to put up.

"I was going to hum," chuckled Dan. "Maybe I'll be inspired to sing if you agree to get dressed up and hear me out over dinner."

"I'm not going around the block with you," BeeGee said in a slightly astonished tone. She got to her feet and hauled the first carton of tiles to the center of the room. "I'm not going anywhere with you, on a date or on a dare."

There wasn't any answer. Silence wasn't like Dan, either. Instead of arguing or kidding her or angrily stomping around, he was sitting there watching her slit open the heavy corrugated box. BeeGee tried to pretend he wasn't there but she was a lousy actress and she knew it. Her quick little sidelong glances were intercepted every time by his unwavering blue eyes.

She began to line up the garish squares along the chalk line indicating the exact center of the kitchen, thinking Dan would leave. Any minute he'd be gone, as swiftly and as devastatingly as he'd come into her world, her life...her heart. BeeGee slapped the tile into place as hard as she could and was aware only of one miserable tear escaping down her cheek.

Wordlessly, Dan took a few tiles and added them to the growing line. Part of her wanted to tell him to stop and get out. There would be no more working together companionably, nothing more he would show her, nothing more they would share. But the other part of BeeGee was wildly happy to be this close once more, whether there was a future or a reason.

"I guess it's settled, then," Dan said quietly after a few minutes. "I'll have to stay."

"I've done plenty of floors myself before," BeeGee murmured huskily.

"I'm not talking about this job, Ruth. I'm referring to you and me. Us. Fort Myers has a new real-estate investor to deal with or a new whatever it takes to make a living here." He rocked back on his heels and suppressed a shudder. BeeGee couldn't tell if it was because of his prospects or the hideous floor.

"You don't mean that!" In her astonishment and disbelief, a whole corner of the flimsy material cracked off in her clutching fingers. "Everything you don't want, Dan? Everything you left behind in Detroit but with palm trees?"

"With you," he said simply.

Mrs. Bleeker squawked shrilly from the other room, demanding to know what was wrong, whom BeeGee was talking to. She bustled in, making disgruntled worried noises. The sight of a strange man and her employee on the kitchen floor, more interested in each other than in her remodeling job, elicited a burst of high-pitched squeals.

"Ten minutes...outside," pleaded Dan. "Am I worth ten minutes, Ruth?"

She shifted her gaze from the lady of the house to him. He was worth this whole kitchen, grotesque tiles and Mrs. Bleeker thrown in for free. He said he would stay. With her. It took a while for that to sink in. She started to laugh, grabbed his hand and they made for the door while Mrs. Bleeker was launching into her speech about Mr. Bleeker's bad temper.

Outside, the sun poured down on them but it was the warmth of Dan's arms and his kisses that melted BeeGee. She didn't care who was looking, who would talk. Holding him again and being held was all that counted.

"Tell me it's you. Tell me it's true…everything you said. You're here. You're here for good!" She was babbling, drowning in the happiness she couldn't repress another second.

"I'll tell you anything, everything…." He lifted her and applied enough pressure to her ribs to force the air out of her lungs in a explosive, joyful cry. "But first…"

His cheek scraped and tickled until his mouth found hers, kissing her over and over with mounting ardor. There didn't seem to be much he could tell her beyond the unbelievable, marvelous message of his kisses. *I love you.* She could hear it as plainly as if he shouted it from the highest tower.

"I'm punchy," he whispered, breathing in the fragrance of her skin. BeeGee mixed with mastic adhesive was his favorite scent. "I've been on the road almost two solid days, Ohio to here. The details can wait. This can't. Are you going to marry me? No, *when* are you going to marry me? You have no option but the date."

"If I say no…" She chewed on his ear playfully, bit a line along his jaw. "I did once, you remember."

"I didn't ask the right way," chuckled Dan. "And you won't let me do it right this time, either. No candlelit dinner, no violins, no grinning idiot of a waiter sneaking up as I sink to one knee…"

"Mrs. Bleeker," grumbled BeeGee, catching sight of the lean, horse-faced figure on the porch. The impatient housewife was fiddling with her dust rag and staring at them malevolently.

"I don't want to marry Mrs. Bleeker. I don't want to go back in there and help you finish her nasty floor but I will. The sooner you get done," promised Dan, "the quicker we can get to the important stuff."

"Like this!" BeeGee kissed him full on the mouth. "Like this!" She hugged him as hard as she could. As they walked back past Mrs. Bleeker, she said in her spriteliest manner, "Two for the price of one, Althea. You are going to have the best tile floor in all of west Florida. And you can tell everyone at my wedding I said so. Meet the mister."

My wedding. My husband. The thoughts that ran through her gave her the chills. She had found a family and a home in one of the strangest ways imaginable. She had met and fallen in love with Dan in an unusual set of circumstances. Why shouldn't he rush in and propose and celebrate a marriage in a totally unorthodox fashion?

They laughed, of course, wrestling tiles from each other and gleefully exchanging gooey smears of glue. They argued loudly about who was the better worker. Mrs. Bleeker was so glad to see them finish without wrecking her kitchen, she shooed them off and insisted she would clean up herself.

BeeGee floated home on Dan's arm. He told her about the trek to Ohio and how empty he'd felt when they'd arrived. He hadn't cared where he was. Without her, another steeple had meant no more than a hill of beans.

He stopped, almost in midstep, and made BeeGee face him. "I thought I was in love once, years ago. I've been using Diane Mather as a shield to keep from loving anyone else since then. But it wasn't love, Ruth. Please look at me, honey, and let me say it."

She blinked hard to keep back the tears that rose when he mentioned a name she didn't want to hear. "I couldn't compete with a memory. She is rich and educated and beautiful."

"And I wouldn't give up anything for her. I wouldn't make a thing she wanted important in my life. I wanted her my way or no way at all. I will have you any way I can get you." Dan saw the doubt creep into her eyes. "Not to have you physically, although too much more waiting will make a wreck of me. To be with you always. To have children with you. To get too old to climb a curb with you."

The tears rolling down her cheeks were the best ones she'd shed. There had been lots of tears in the past ten days but all cried in secret, in the darkness of her room, and out of the misery of loneliness. She wasn't ashamed of the ones she wept now from the fullness of love.

"You're sure?" she choked between sobs. "After less than two months? I'm afraid to believe this is real."

"You'll believe it," Dan said firmly. "I'll make you believe it with a nice white wedding and a honeymoon on Sanibel Island. You'll believe it when we call Alex and Judy tonight and tell them when to fly down for the festivities. If you don't ask Judy to be matron of honor, you better believe she'll never talk to you again for as long as we both shall live."

Her eyes sparkled and she danced along, trying to keep up with Dan's quick strides. "And Kip as ring bearer. And...and...and..." There were so many sweet details to plan and savor to make a dream become real.

Doc and Emma didn't turn a hair when Dan Greening appeared for dinner and announced he was staying forever. Not with them, he hastily amended. For all the surprise they showed, a prospective son-in-law might drop in every other day. Their happiness was evident, though, and BeeGee drank in the sight of the people she loved gathered together.

Doc talked sense. Dan talked about real estate and the new condominium and vacation-time-share markets in Florida. Emma rattled on about the utter madness of getting a wedding dress and planning a decent reception in less than a month or two.

"A week," interjected Dan, without losing his place in his conversation with Doc. "It better be a week or less or..."

"Or what?" challenged BeeGee.

Dan's knee pressed hers under the table. He leaned forward and assumed a solemn expression. Under the tablecloth's cover, his leg stretched and moved along hers. She could feel herself getting pink and warm.

"Let's see. I could change my mind and call that Swedish actress who keeps sending me letters in purple ink. Or I could get busy in a few weeks at a new job and make money to support my bride."

Money was not an issue, Dan had assured her earlier. He was going to tell Alex tonight to sell the small trailer and there was more than enough in Dan's bank account to make a down payment on a house. BeeGee had a pretty good notion of why Dan wasn't willing to wait too long. At least, her body was sending and receiving some very potent signals. A long engagement seemed like a terrible idea, when the short time before she and Dan could politely excuse themselves from the table was already dragging painfully.

"You two go make that call to Ohio. I'll run and fluff up the pillows in the spare bedroom for Dan," instructed Emma. She fixed her stern eye on Dan. "I won't abide any motel-hotel talk. Family is family, and family stays here."

"I'll try not to sleepwalk," teased Dan with a glance at BeeGee.

"Not to worry," growled Doc. "I'll slip sleeping pills in your coffee every night. I'll patrol the hallway. I'll tie you hand and foot to the bed with gauze bandages." He beamed and broke into laughter. "Or I'll just remember why Emma and I kept changing our wedding date, moving it up, until we were pointed at and whispered about. I do believe every person we met those first nine months talked directly to Em's stomach and counted under his breath."

"Doc!" Emma's voice reverberated through the entire house. "Don't you dare let them think what they're thinking right this minute! Leonard was born ten months to the day after our wedding."

BeeGee was seized with a fit of hysterical giggles, most unusual for her. She was, so to speak, their baby but she was hardly sheltered or stupid. There was something humorous about picturing Emma Alden nearly half a century younger and nearly wicked.

It was a night for laughter and tears. Judy blubbered over the phone into BeeGee's ear, jumbling her congratulations with an oath that she would wear any color but yellow. She did not want to appear as a banana with a bulge, she said emphatically. According to Judy, the only thing that could make her happier than seeing Dan and BeeGee married would be to have the baby in Fort Myers the same day. Then, no one would forget the occasion.

When Alex and Dan talked, BeeGee grew uneasy. There wasn't much to overhear with Dan giving short answers and many "uh-huhs." She pushed the feeling away with distaste. Alex was happy. He told her so and twitted her about being the first woman who could bring Dan back to earth.

Chapter Ten

A whirlwind romance could only produce a hurricane wedding. The following days were so hectic there wasn't much time to think. Blood tests and licenses were almost minor items down at the bottom of a huge list taped to Em's refrigerator. BeeGee hurried out of the house each morning armed with a hastily scribbled assignment sheet and stumbled back each evening to compare notes with Dan about their accomplishments. They cuddled and swung together on the glider, exhausted.

Dan was reciting the firms he visited. "Richter and Lowe, Vista Mar Developers, Sea Stars Condos...."

His prospects looked very good. Two of the three men who interviewed him this week were willing to let him start on whatever date he named. They were gung ho, seeing Dan and his résumé, but Dan didn't sound particularly enamored of any of the men or the firms. In spite of his reservations, he said he would make a decision over the weekend. "And buy a new suit," he added.

"Suit, suit," shouted BeeGee, roused from her stupor. "I almost forgot." You have to schedule a final fitting for your tux tomorrow. Before or after we meet to pick up our rings?"

"In between," laughed Dan. "We also pick up Judy and Alex and Kip tomorrow, go look at another house, see the minister and, for all I know, consult the astrologer to check if the day we picked is auspicious."

"You hate this, don't you?" BeeGee picked her head up off his shoulder and butted him playfully in the chest. "Go on, admit it! I got to vent my spleen about the dress, being poked, pinched and stuck with pins. I hate being told I should let out a first-Communion dress instead of buying a wedding gown and having them take it in."

"I hate the fuss and the frenzy," Dan said honestly, "but I love you. And this has got to be as nearly perfect a wedding as it can be, whatever it takes."

She sighed and settled back in his arms. The wedding might or might not be perfect. There were too many things to do in too short a time but she didn't care. Their marriage would be a perfect and lasting union, which was what she really valued. She kept that thought foremost in her mind, telling herself that the daily untangling of snags over which house was best or affordable, which job Dan took or which dress fit was secondary.

She had everything. Her favorite dreams as a little girl had been of true love, a big family, a real home. They had come true and were still coming true, not always smoothly but in a grander way than she had envisioned. Her childhood had been rich in fantasies and little else, but she knew, when Dan was holding her like this, she would never be poor, frightened or alone again.

"I didn't like the setup at Richter and Lowe," Dan was muttering, debating aloud. "The salary-commission-and-bonus package sounds great but there's no energy, no spark to them. What do you think? Should I go for the gold?"

BeeGee made a noncommittal reply. His job, his choice. What about his dreams, she thought with a guilty twinge. No investment firm was an energetic and lively as steeplejacking. No boss was going to be the way Dan and Alex had been, freewheeling and carefree, easygoing and hardworking. It took effort to shake the uneasiness she felt.

"Carry me upstairs and put me in bed," she said wearily. "I know how brazen that sounds but I don't think either of us is in any condition to act on it."

"Really?" Dan slung her over his shoulder like a small sack of potatoes, paying no attention to her howling that this was not quite what she had in mind. "Thanks," he said when her kicks opened the door for them both. "Hope you cooperate like this when I put your pj's on."

"Down," BeeGee shrieked as he jostled her on every step. "Down, put me down..."

"Need help?" Doc's voice rang out, and from her peculiar upside-down view, BeeGee waved feebly at him and nodded assent.

"Nope, I see you've got it under control," Doc said, vanishing back into his bedroom.

Unceremoniously, Dan dumped her on her own bed and whipped off her shoes. The socks went next, with a pause to tickle the soles of her feet. When she was writhing and helpless with laughter, Dan pinned her down and his fingers wrought more havoc along her ribs, under her arms, until he fumbled with buttons at the waistband of her shorts.

"You wouldn't dare," sputtered BeeGee. "Omigosh..."

"You're right," Dan sighed. He rested on her, keeping most of his weight on his arms. "I wouldn't dare. I'm not going to start anything I can't finish, but watch out! It will be one of the most special occasions of my life when we really do belong to each other." He grazed his lips across her mouth and nibbled lightly on her ear. "Beware of a crazed maniac on our honeymoon."

"I'm scared to death," she kidded, her eyes shining up at him. "Does insanity run in your family?"

"You bet." He proceeded to move and touch and kiss her for a brief moment calculated to drive them both close to the edge of sanity. "And I want to live dangerously."

"You said you wouldn't start..." muttered BeeGee, but her voice was weak and insincere. When Dan sat up next to her, she was disappointed. He was smiling.

"How pretty you look," he whispered. "How great it's going to be to see you next to me every morning. I bragged so extravagantly about you to my dad that he made me swear I'd send him some pictures this week. Oh, Lord, there's one more thing to add to our list!"

"Your dad. Your mother. Your parents!" Bee-Gee's face twisted with the sudden thought of the older couple she had seen only in a photograph. In these tumultuous days of preparation, she'd given no thought to his family, other than Alex and Judy and Kip. "Dan, they know but they won't be here...oh, I feel awful."

"There's just my father and he can't fly in for the wedding. I called him, Ruth, and told him all about you. He isn't able to travel much. He isn't going to be here but I promised we'd get to Michigan on our first vacation."

She kept her hands balled into tight fists, feeling the sharp edges of her nails scoring her palms. She didn't know Dan's mother had died several years ago. She didn't know his father was sick or anything else about her prospective father-in-law. Dan didn't act disturbed but BeeGee let out some of her own guilt and grief.

"I feel like a brat," she said. "How could I forget you have parents, relatives, hordes of family? I keep thinking, 'Me, mine.' I'm wrapped up in what's happening to me, not you."

"What's happening to *us*," corrected Dan. He unfolded her fingers and kissed each mark she'd left on her palms. "Ruth, everything will sort itself out. It's too rough trying to squeeze our whole lives into a few weeks. It's impossible to compress every basic fact into a tiny pill we can each take to learn everything about each other. Maybe that's why I wasn't a believer in love at first sight but I am now. It's going to work."

"We'll visit your father first chance we get," she said tearfully. "And before we go, I'll know the name of the street you lived on, what schools you went to, what colors you like, what vegetables you won't eat."

Dan arranged himself next to her, full-length on the white-and-pink-checked spread, with his head on the eyelet-trimmed pillow. He looked incongruous but neither of them laughed. BeeGee burrowed closer and let him stroke her back, kiss her forehead.

"My dad retired from the railroad," began Dan, as if he was reciting a bedtime story for Kip. "I always wondered if Alex and I got the itch to travel from his stories about where the trains went. I was born the day after Thanksgiving and I'm allergic to cats. Alex shot me with a BB gun when I was seven."

"Where?" hiccoughed BeeGee.

"You can see the spot—there's no scar—after we're married," chuckled Dan. "The humiliation of having the pellet removed almost killed me."

As she listened, she learned much more than how repulsive brussels sprouts were to him. How open, how easily Dan could talk about his boyhood and adolescence! He wasn't afraid to tell BeeGee about any aspect of his past and he didn't spare himself when he mentioned mistakes or failures.

Listening to Dan, BeeGee reveled in an intimacy as great as physical closeness. He had become her friend, soon he would be her lover, but tonight she was his confidante. There would be lots of nights like this, she hoped. Nights and days to trade feelings and thoughts that no one else would hear. It was wonderful to have a lifetime to look, to listen, to sort things out.

"Look. Look out the window," directed BeeGee, nudging Dan in the ribs.

The bedside lamp could be switched off. The sun was beginning to glow above the windowsill and they were still talking.

"Another sleepless night," Dan said, nuzzling her. "I didn't mind this one, though. At least I wasn't pacing the carpet next door or chewing the plaster in frustration."

"Let's do it again soon," suggested BeeGee, tugging on his hand. "But not too soon or I'll snore through the ceremony."

The arrival of the Greenings heightened the madness but gave BeeGee new energy. Judy didn't stop pouring marital advice into BeeGee's ear at every opportunity. Kip raced around the Aldens' house, strutting proudly in his first suit or "helping" Em prepare goodies for the reception. Alex and Dan held peculiar conversations in a brother-to-brother shorthand that puzzled BeeGee. At the first opportunity she cornered Dan to break the code.

"What's the mumbling about?" she demanded. "Is everything all right?"

Dan evaded the questions at first.

"With us? Fine! You know my brother thinks you're aces."

"Dan! I saw his face while you two were talking. He's upset, worried. Alex doesn't usually scowl. He didn't even eat much...."

She was almost sorry she was so persistent when, bit by bit, Dan told her the whole story. The Dayton job was proving too big for Alex to handle solo; he was facing a default on the contract. The likeliest solution was for him to find and train some local people to steeplejack when they returned to Ohio. Alex wasn't very optimistic, however. His tentative search so far hadn't turned up any potential mountain goats. Steeplejacks were a scarce commodity.

Dan didn't say he felt personally responsible for Alex's bind. He didn't have to. BeeGee saw the struggle in his face and heard the underlying note of hopelessness. From now on, Alex would have to pick and choose carefully to avoid taking on more than he could handle alone.

"Does he resent us?" BeeGee asked uncomfortably. "I wish there was something we could do...."

"Alex doesn't resent or regret anything. He and Judy practically booted me into the Bronco when I told them what I wanted to do. Ask him yourself if you have any doubts."

She didn't ask. There never seemed to be enough time. The conversation nagged at her but there were other loose ends to tie up. She wanted to start her new life without any problems or strings attached. The wedding was two days away.

Lost in the froth of white lace, ribbons and roses, BeeGee's fingers were trembling. She thought her voice might shake, too, when it came time for her to speak the few binding words. It was emotion, not nervousness or doubt. It was too much love to be contained.

Emma was in her element, calmly running the show. She snapped one last picture of BeeGee in front of the church, her face lifted to catch a final peek at the steeple. "Don't fuss with the bouquet. Don't gawk. You picked this church."

"I wouldn't want my wedding anywhere else," said BeeGee.

Em handed the camera to Doc. She busied herself adjusting the veil over the very last of the Alden brides, the newest of her daughters. The finest tulle didn't hide any of the glow of the tiny oval face beneath it. A bale of netting wouldn't have disguised or dimmed the light in Ruth Ellen Chambers's eyes.

Em glanced nervously over her shoulder to check and see if Doc was out of earshot. "Honey, it takes only one thing besides love to make a marriage. Not money, not luck, not even health. Courage. Raw, ol' come-what-may courage. Think about it!"

"Mother," Doc called sternly, "the minister is signaling us. Do not take this opportunity to ask our girl if she flossed her teeth or took her vitamins."

BeeGee threw her arms around Emma and hugged her, mindless of wrinkles and the gesturing minister. "I know, Mom. That's why I wanted it here. This little church is all about courage, especially mine."

She probably could never fully explain to herself or anyone else the ironic and poetic meaning this church had, but she held on to certain memories of pride and terror and wonder inspired here.

The minister had been thrilled by the reappearance of the very people who'd labored to make his modest church sounder and lovelier. Dr. Hampton, perhaps, guessed why BeeGee had rejected the grander, larger church in town for the humble First Baptist. It was more appropriate to be here, to be reminded without a sermon of how precarious life could be and how swiftly events occurred that changed its course.

She wanted very much to remember every detail of this day but it was impossible. There were too many images to collect and store during the brief ceremony.

There were too many faces to recognize in the crowded interior. The scent of flowers in the hot, heavy air of late summer was overpowering. The choir sang but she heard Doc sniffling with sentiment into his handkerchief. The minister began to read, appropriately, from the Book of Ruth.

"'Whither thou goest, I will go; and where thou lodgest...'"

The sight of Dan's blue eyes turned to her blotted out everything else. How proud and confident he looked. How fearless and sure he sounded when his "I do" rang out.

For a fraction of a second, when Dan slipped the plain wide band on her finger, BeeGee got the heart-stopping sensation she had forgotten something. What had she overlooked? What had she ignored? She strained to hold the thought but it faded with the kiss Dan gave her, washed away in a flood of happiness. It was over and it was perfect; she was Mrs. Daniel Greening.

Later, in the crush of embracing guests, amid the din of congratulations, BeeGee was caught off her guard by the same nagging feeling. A beginning also marked an ending, bittersweet and poignant. Alex and Judy and Kip would not be staying; they had a plane to catch and goodbyes to say. In a single day, she had acquired more family and was parting from them. The inevitability of loss did not make it any easier.

"They'll be fine," Dan told her as they waved to his family. "You didn't cry at the wedding. This is no time to start. You know the Greenings now, and we might stumble..."

"But you never fall," finished BeeGee, taking his arm. "You always land on your feet. I know, I'm one of you, after all. They'll do fine, I'm sure."

She would ignore the huskiness in his voice if Dan would tactfully disregard the misting in the corners of her eyes. She smiled up at him and concentrated on the future, not the past—his or hers.

They drove and checked into one of the island's brand-new luxury motels. It was late. The Aldens' reception had been lovely but long. The tables had been stripped of food and the last champagne bottle emptied hours before the guests were ready to leave. She and Dan must have tried to make a discreet exit ten times before they succeeded.

Dan signed the register with a flourish: Mr. and Mrs. D. Greening, Fort Myers. "Hungry? I think Mario's is still open," he said innocently to BeeGee.

"Oh, yes. Until midnight," supplied the desk clerk helpfully.

She wanted to laugh and punch Dan at the same time. It was impossible to remember when she had last eaten as much as a saltine, but a four-course meal was not high on her list of priorities. Unless she was sadly mistaken, the expression on Dan's face meant appetite for other fare, too.

"Their shrimp will wait. This shrimp won't," she said, perfectly straight-faced.

Their room was probably beautiful with a magnificent view of the ocean, but BeeGee would have to wait until morning to find out. Dan wouldn't turn on the light or let her pull the heavy draperies leading to their balcony. He pushed their luggage inside the door and went to turn down the bed.

"Don't move," he ordered, and BeeGee stood there.

He came back to her to put his arms around her gently, to ruffle her hair lovingly. "You know an old family ritual," he whispered, "and we'll start there. Then we proceed to learn a new family ritual with years and years to practice and perfect it."

She wanted to learn everything he could teach her. Nobody could be more patient, she thought dazedly, or more wonderful. Every kiss Dan gave her was unhurried, as leisurely and long as she needed to allow any shreds of shyness or fear to vanish. Clinging to him, answering the growing urgency of his mouth, BeeGee felt her impatience building to know, to belong, to surrender completely to him.

"We're not going to stand here all night, are we?" she pleaded weakly. His hands didn't stop doing things that made her senses reel.

"Only until I fall down or faint," Dan hummed in her ear. "Any second now." He tugged at his clothing, undressing himself faster than she thought it was humanly possible to do, but when he reached for her, it was in slow motion again.

Even as his fingers slipped buttons through button-holes and carefully took off every item she was wearing, he was making love to her. Dan said things she hadn't imagined she would ever hear; she hadn't known words could arouse and excite as much as his lingering touch did.

"Look at me, Ruth," he commanded softly. "There's not going to be anything secret or shameful between us, nothing hidden, nothing forbidden."

His hands moved on her bare skin, warmly, surely. Dan stepped back to let their eyes caress each other. He was beautiful, fiercely and awesomely beautiful, and she felt free to tell him so. Her arms rose, opened to welcome him.

"Flattery will get you..." Dan said, and paused to lift her, "...right into bed."

He was next to her, whispering and showing her how much he loved her. She was not surprised by the depth of his tenderness or the sweet, gentle exploration he led her through. The only surprise was the wildness Dan released in her each time he allowed her to answer his question. "Do you like this?"

"Yes, yes," she heard herself saying until the answers became her moans of pleasure and his questions the sound of ragged breathing. With their unbearable excitement, there was no pain or it dissolved quickly into the delight of mutual discovery. Unafraid, she let herself climb higher and higher with each new sensation until there was nothing but them in the universe at heights she didn't think existed, and then the dizzying, breathtaking plummet back to earth in his arms.

She held him tightly for a long time in the darkness, content to be quiet. The slow, lazy stroke of Dan's fingers along the length of her back calmed her but kept her floating above the sea of sleep.

"Worth the wait?" he inquired softly. "I hope I'm not a disappointment to you but I'll keep trying until I get better."

Her fingertips traced the smile on his lips and moved on, shamelessly copying the patterns he was drawing on her damp skin. Waiting was over and she shifted languidly under the kisses he was still eager to give, still rich with hunger. If there was any disappointment, it was that this night wouldn't last forever. "Sometimes," BeeGee suggested boldly, "more is better."

She had made a terrible mistake. She woke, unable to avoid the conclusion any longer.

BeeGee propped herself up in bed, arranging the pillows and smoothing the wrinkles in the crisp white acres of linen around her. The full realization of her error had not struck quickly like a venomous snake; it had been growing for a while and that morning, her second day as a married woman, it blossomed, a mysterious full-blown flower—very beautiful, very toxic if she let it grow another day.

Dan was not next to her. She knew exactly where he was—jogging on the white beach outside to keep himself in shape. He hated exercise; he had confided as much to her the night they talked in her own twin bed. Exercise was artificial but he felt he had to begin some kind of regimen to keep fit. Investment brokers didn't do the hard physical work of steeplejacks, and Dan, kidding and tickling her, had confessed he wanted BeeGee to find him attractive, physically beautiful, for as long as humanly possible. Flat stomach, lean and muscular body and the strength of Hercules.

"You should have run with me," gasped Dan. "Tomorrow you will. I want to wheeze my last breath in your arms."

She laughed, watching him strip off his sweat-soaked clothes and hustle away to the shower. But the laughter was poisoned by her thought. BeeGee got up and talked above the water's noise, enjoying her view of Dan through the frosted glass door.

"What's on our agenda for today?"

Dan flicked soapsuds over the divider at her. "Fooling around, breakfast, swim, fooling around, lunch and then, who knows? Maybe," he chuckled to himself, "some fooling around."

"Excuse me," she shouted. "I'm going to lie down and rest up for the fooling around."

Chewing on her fingernail, BeeGee dropped back into the bed. She sorted through her thoughts as if she was dealing out cards. Honeymoons don't last forever and their honeymoon wasn't any different. She and Dan were having the time of their lives but Judy and Alex were on their way back to disaster. She missed them. Dan hadn't mentioned them since they left but she knew he was thinking about them, wondering what was going to happen with Alex's plans.

Her fingers went to her throat to toy with Dan's special gift to her. No engagement ring, BeeGee had insisted. She wasn't the diamond type and it wasn't practical to plaster walls and trowel cement flashing a diamond ring. Dan disagreed with half of her argument. At the reception, he put the necklace on her without comment. BeeGee rubbed the tiny gold Eiffel Tower, topped with a diamond, for courage, for inspiration and for love.

"I want to call Judy," she said to her towel-clad husband.

Dan scurried over, dripping water on her, to hold the phone receiver in the cradle. "Ruth, if you call at this time of the morning on the second day of our honeymoon, she'll think something's wrong."

"Something's wrong," BeeGee said with conviction.

"Oh, babe," he crooned, "what could be wrong? We're in heaven. This is a dream." He was out of the towel and slipping into the bed next to her before she could answer.

"My dream," murmured BeeGee between kisses. "Not much of yours, mostly mine."

His hands were moving over her, eager to prove this was his dream, too. But she wanted to tell him what she meant. She'd given up nothing and got everything she ever wanted with this man. Dan was the one who'd left his family, his work, his home to make her happy. She'd fallen in love with Dan for the very qualities she was asking him to suppress—his independent, restless nature, his ability to be his own man.

"You're not going to like Richter and Lowe," she said before he could distract her completely.

"They're bozos...but rich bozos. I'll learn to like them."

"I doubt that. You're not going to like working for someone else, are you?" She put her hand on his shoulder, seeing the flash of gold from her wedding ring. It was the symbol of permanence—without beginning, without end—between them but she could not see Dan as a twenty-year man with Richter and Lowe. Her whole life had been a search for permanency; Dan's life headed him for freedom. An eagle with clipped wings was still a bird. It still yearned to fly.

When his head lifted and the kisses ceased, she knew the answers before he spoke. The rings they wore were only symbolic; the real gold was not just a charm on her necklace or a band on her finger. The truly lasting gold had to be mined from their love and it was her turn to dig deep within herself.

"This is serious. Whatever it is, it's really bothering you," Dan said, stroking the little creases in her forehead.

"In a couple of years, you'll resent being tied down here. You'll always wonder, what if we had done this or that, what if we had pulled the fat out of the fire for Alex..." She rushed on, afraid to stop talking, because she was tempted to back down.

To Dan's credit, he didn't deny it. He didn't try to hush her but instead appeared to ponder the idea. No quick answers, no pat reassurances. He listened.

Courage, Emma had counseled. It took courage to change, to break open and grow. BeeGee understood what Emma meant now and she hung grimly on to her insight, refusing to push it into the back of her mind just because it frightened her. Dan was ready, willing and able to sacrifice what he was to become hers. Was she ready to change, to compromise? Did she have his courage?

"You know I liked steeplejacking," she continued. "I liked Sarasota, too. I guess I was brave enough to climb the tower but not brave enough to look around from the top."

"Huh?" asked Dan succinctly. "What in the Sam Hill...?"

"I made a mistake. I think there's time to rectify it."

"Honey, I don't know what you're talking about," protested Dan, "but we'll work it out. Together. Now, start making sense."

"You taught me all about the highest tower, about steeplejacking, about...oh, never mind," said BeeGee, breaking into laughter as his concern transformed into total bewilderment. "It'll take too long to explain."

She launched herself at him, using the direct approach—another thing he'd taught her—to show him she was relieved and happy, not leading up to anything dire. The weight that held her down for so long lifted even as Dan was lifting her to fit her to himself.

Climbing the highest tower and standing at the pinnacle was only the beginning. Their real work was cut out for them. From this new height, BeeGee saw the vastness and complexity of the world and two lives twined together. From the vantage point of love, she'd realized it could never be all her way or all his way again. Exposed to strong winds of change and the lightning strokes of fate, they would have to brave the storms, willing to compromise and move up and down. It was not only their work that would make them a team; it was their commitment.

"Wait...wait a second," whispered Dan, a trifle breathless from her attack. "This feels great but I still don't know what we're working out—besides our muscles."

"I'll tell you all about my marvelous insight on the plane," promised BeeGee.

"What plane? We have three more days here...."

She shook her head vigorously from side to side. "We have to get to Ohio before Alex sells our home. We have to get busy on that job. He'll never find anyone as good as we are."

The sheer joy and the relief that crossed his face proved to her that she was right.

"You're not kidding," Dan shouted gleefully. "Tell me you're not kidding."

She picked up the bedside phone and informed the desk that the Greenings would be checking out at noon. "Here are the terms," she continued after hanging up. "Two, maybe three yearly trips back to Florida to check on Doc and Em. That'll reassure me I haven't abandoned them or lost my way. Goofy or not, I need that. My God, travel will run into money, won't it?"

"We can manage," Dan said, with a smile splitting his face.

"After the children arrive . . ."

He slapped his forehead. "Not so fast. Are you trying to hint at something else?"

BeeGee snorted. "Not yet. But when we begin to expand operations, so to speak, we'll sit down and re-negotiate. Okay? I have to be convinced that it's really healthy to bring up kids on a migratory route. By that time, Alex may have a restaurant, anyway. I can learn to cook, if my life depends on it."

She wriggled out of his arms and swung her feet over the edge of the bed. Dan snagged her around the waist and hauled her back against him.

"I'm so glad you decided to consult me," he purred, snaking his hand over the soft, unresisting length of her. "Anything else we haven't covered?"

"Just packing and tickets and telling Richter and Lowe, Doc and Em . . ." She went on and on until he bit her playfully on the nape of the neck. Then she laughed softly and turned to pull Dan down to her. "Actually, I can think of a thousand things, but checkout isn't until noon. It'll be close but if anyone can do it . . ."

"BeeGee can," Dan whispered. And his mouth met hers to seal a brave and lasting bond.

You won't want to miss a single one of the heartfelt stories presented by Silhouette Special Edition; and when you take advantage of this special offer, you won't have to.

You'll also receive a FREE subscription to the Silhouette Books Newsletter as long as you remain a member. Each lively issue is filled with news on upcoming titles, interviews with your favorite authors, even their favorite recipes.

To become a home subscriber and receive your first 4 books FREE, fill out and mail the coupon today!

Silhouette Special Edition®

Silhouette Romance

COMING NEXT MONTH

SOUND OF SUMMER—Annette Broadrick
As star of the TV series "Derringer Drake," Selena was used to daring adventure—but not on her vacation! Meeting Adam Conroy ensured that this would be a trip she'd never forget.

SWEET SEA SPIRIT—Emilie Richards
Sandy doubted that a dignified lawyer like Tyler could fall in love with a free-spirited tomboy, but she was also a professional. If only she could prove it to him....

BEFORE THE LOVING—Beverly Terry
Peri Brendan's organizational skills landed her a job in Mexico. Handling her new employer's family crisis was not part of the job description, but then again, neither was falling in love.

SHADOW CHASING—Debbie Macomber
Carla had decided to have a casual fling on vacation in Mazatlán, but Philip was not a man to be taken lightly. Beneath the Mexican sun, temperatures began to rise.

LOVERS' REUNION—Terri Herrington
Although their marriage had ended two years before, Cassie and Sly played the happy couple for their high-school reunion, not realizing that the charade might expose the true yearning in their hearts.

THE COURTSHIP OF DANI—Ginna Gray
Dani had brains and beauty, a combination that many people had tried to exploit. Was Jason St. Clair earnest in his courtship, or did he have ulterior motives, too?

AVAILABLE NOW:

AFTER THE MUSIC Diana Palmer	**HEART SHIFT** Glenda Sands
FAMILY SECRETS Ruth Langan	**THE CATNIP MAN** Barbara Turner
THE HIGHEST TOWER Ann Hurley	**MINE BY WRITE** Marie Nicole